The Unknown Watchman

The Flight and Survival of a Child Soldier in Occupied Europe

Tammy C. Ferris

SDC Publishing, LLC was established to promote and encourage aspiring writers and artists. It is a family oriented vehicle through which they can publish their work.
Contact SDC Publishing, LLC at allenfmahon@gmail.com
Or on the web at SDCPublishingLLC.com

Tammy C. Ferris

While the events of this account were documented through personal interviews and personal records shared at the writing of this book, it is not meant to give a strict account of specific places, timelines or living persons. It is intended only to create a story line of what child soldiers of Europe may have experienced in WWII. The opinions expressed in this work are those of the author and not of the publisher or any living person. It is a work of fiction with the hopes of giving due respect to the many allies of Polish descent who served their nation well.

The opinions expressed in this manuscript are solely the opinions of the author and do not represent the opinions or thoughts of the publisher. The author has represented and warranted full ownership and/or legal right to publish all the materials in this book.

The Unknown Watchman

SDC Publishing, LLC

ISBN: 1718638957
ISBN-13: 978-1718638952

Tammy C. Ferris

DEDICATION

I dedicate this book, first and foremost, to the One Who sees all and directs the steps of man regardless of the plans man makes.
It is only in obedience to Him that I share this work.
His name is El-Roi, the God Who sees (Genesis 16:13).

This story is also dedicated to the often forgotten Polish soldiers and citizens of WWII who proudly served their beloved nation. Special dedication goes to my "child soldier" friend who willingly shared his personal experiences of war to educate others of the war-time sacrifices made by Polish children of WWII.
May their love and sacrifice for Poland truly never be forgotten.

Tammy C. Ferris

ACKNOWLEDGMENTS

A heartfelt thank you goes to Almighty God Who directed me to write a book I never intended to write. Yet, it was through my desire to be obedient to Him that finally brought about my acceptance of this project. Only He alone is aware of "great and mighty things which thou knowest not" (Jeremiah 33:3) pertaining to this work. My job is simply to be obedient.

Next, I thank my husband, Jerry, whose belief that I could write a book got the wheels turning. I thank him for his constant love, encouragement and support even when I dragged my feet.

Thank you to my family and close friends (especially Donna, Emmy, Wanda and Laura) who believed in this project, prayed for it and shared their enthusiasm.

A loving thank you goes to my late 95-year-old mother who always wanted to see her daughter "write a book." (I'm sorry you aren't here, Mama, to see it finally become a reality, but maybe you do know.)

Thank you to John Wiley (author of "I Will Build" biography series and "A Brief History of Virginia) who was kindly willing to edit this book in its earliest stages. Also, thank you to Laura Selkirk who applied her expertise as an English teacher to do the detailed work of the final editing of this project. Thank you, John and Laura, for your love of history and the written language. You've played an important part in my personal obedience to God.

A special thank you, to Dorothy Etzler Barnett, a talented artist of Botetourt County, Virginia. The sacrificial hours she spent on research and design captured the very essence of this book.

Next, many thanks to Stephen, Donovan Carson Publishing of Buchanan, VA who gave the opportunity for "life" to a manuscript believed to be long dead. God bless you. Most of all…to GOD be the glory! After all, it really is His story!

Prelude

The dark-haired girl cautiously walked to the end of the gangplank where she set her worn leather suitcase against the railing, the only thing in this brand new world she could call her own. She paused a moment to adjust her traveling hat firmly in place as the ocean breeze played with its brim. If only she could regain her "land legs." She swayed precariously, willing the dizziness, born of too many days on the high seas, to stop. Unfortunately, her brain wasn't listening.

The girl tilted her head back, closed her eyes and slowly breathed in the air which still smelled of salt. Would she ever lose that distinctive odor or would it be imbedded in her head forever? Whatever the case, she had bigger fish to fry at the moment.

Slowly opening her eyes, the girl squinted in the sun and made out the image of the Statue of Liberty, confirmation she was standing on American soil. Sighing, she quickly made the sign of the cross, a practice, or rather a habit, that had long ago been instilled in her. Besides, she took great pride in being a "good Catholic girl" and she was truly grateful that God did allow her to reach her destination. After all, wasn't it only two nights ago that a northeastern storm made her seek out a priest just in case last rites should be administered?

She shook her head and felt a tremble surge through her body. At the tender age of thirteen she had a lot of plans under her belt, those of which included a career, marriage and if God deemed it so, children. But right now she simply wanted to find an aunt she'd never met and a plate of food – as long as it wasn't fish. The husband and career would simply have to wait.

Chapter 1
Of Boy Scouts and Orphans

"Hey, Aleksy," called Koby. "Come help me tie this knot!"

"Koby, I've shown you a hundred times how to tie that thing."

"So, I'm a slow learner; come help me."

Aleksy stood up from the assortment of gear he was plundering through and approached his friend. "Here, let me see what you're doing," he said reaching for the rope. "Good grief, Koby! It's just a square not. How did you get it in such a mess?"

"The rope is too bulky. I can't get it to hold."

"You've got to remember that it's right over left like this," Aleksy demonstrated, "then left over right."

"You make it look easy."

Aleksy tossed the rope back to his friend. "It is easy, Koby. It's the easiest knot you can tie. How do you expect to get your badge if you can't make it past this?"

Koby shrugged. "I don't care about a badge, Aleksy. I just want to go fishing."

Aleksy laughed at his friend. That was Koby all right. All about the fun, not the work. He often wondered why his friend had even become part of the scouts but then realized not joining up would bring shame to his nationalistic parents. As for Aleksy, he would do whatever it took to keep his father off his back. Sometimes he wondered if the man had been sorry Aleksy had ever been born as the boy often felt he could do nothing right.

Aleksy was only fourteen. And the thing that mattered most to him would no longer be what mattered to all boys of his age and era: things like marbles and movies, acting out adventures such as those of Juro Janosik, the Polish equal to Robin Hood, and of course, a little spending money. No, Aleksander Rostek would soon give little thought to childish pleasures as more pressing things would soon vie for *his* attention. Things such as military orders, food, when and where he'd find it, the understanding of foreign tongues, and of course, escape. Mainly survival.

The nightmare began to snake its way from Germany into his native Poland well before the boy's birth. It was conceived in the very pit of Hell and would eventually be unleashed on millions of innocents. What began in the mind of one very troubled man would end in the graves of a multitude from various nations. Adolf Hitler would control the minds of many a German youth, but he would not control the mind of one Polish boy who would even don the Hitler-Jugend uniform in the name of survival.

It all began in a little village on September 1, 1939, when young Aleksander Rostek was busy serving as a Boy Scout messenger with the Civil Defense, as a result of the Nazi invasion against Czechoslovakia the year before. Many young Polish boys, encouraged by their parents, had enlisted in the scouts, putting feet to their patriotic calling. Of course, the promise of camping expeditions, stirred the adventurous heart of Aleksander or "Aleksy" as his friends liked to call him. However, these adolescent boys were far removed from the real-life survival course on which they would soon embark.

Aleksy and Koby had little to no idea of what scouting in Poland was about to entail, although it was understood that boy scouts would immediately be transformed into young soldiers should the battle cry sound. Meanwhile, scouts abroad would have been clueless to such an idea. While other boys throughout the world were continuing the tradition of campfires, preparing meals without utensils and the traditional skills of knot tying, Aleksy and his friends would soon face the greatest challenge of all: protection of country, family and self. The Boy Scouts of WWII Europe would go beyond the usual call of duty. After all, wasn't that the way of patriotism? At least that's how Aleksy and his friends had been raised to see it; so, they dreamed of heroic accolades, including pretty girls fawning over "boy soldiers" upon their return from battle. There were plenty of black and white films in the local theater to attest to this, and besides, a boy had to dream.

Aleksy took his oath of duty to God and his country as well as to think of others and not himself. Thus, when the idea of "underground" scouts would eventually be introduced to him, Aleksy would deem this adventure a worthy one in spite of its dangers.

All along it had been obvious that Aleksander's own parents were supportive to the very point of doing whatever it took to defeat the Germans, even if it meant their own boy being conscripted into the armed services at an early age. Aleksy was aware that this line of thought came more so from his father than from his mother, for she knew her place and remained submissive to her husband. So, it was no wonder the boys of Poland grew up playing war games with their parents' blessings. And from where did this confidence stem? Why, from the Polish success against the Nazis in 1938 when they had run the Germans out of a Polish district in Czechoslovakia.

"Aleksy," his father had said the day his son joined the scouts, "you are more than a Boy Scout. You are a soldier."

Aleksy grinned with pride as his mother smiled. His father was often hard on the boy. If being a soldier meant finally winning his father's approval, so be it. And now Aleksy was about to embark upon his first scouting adventure, and his usually no-nonsense father wanted to take a picture of his son in uniform.

Standing erect, the young "soldier" struck a pose and beamed into the small box style Brownie camera. He waited patiently while his father snapped the photo. "This will be good practice, son, in case we need to run the Nazis off again just as we did last year in Czechoslovakia."

Aleksy had nodded, thinking all he *really* wanted to do, like Koby, was go camping and fishing. He wasn't out to chase Adolf Hitler's armies. After all, at that time, he first joined the scouts, he was only twelve and content to leave the battles to the old men who started them anyway.

Still, as time passed, and the boys grew in their skills of scouting, they were quick to agree that they could take on the Nazis if necessary, just like their fathers before them. They weren't the least bit afraid of a bunch of wolves wearing "coal scuttle" buckets on their heads. At least that's how they joked about it. Aleksy smirked at the very thought and often spent time sketching out cartoons of this rather hilarious rendition of the enemy. Needless to say, his war-loving father delighted in every cartoon directing sarcasm toward the much hated Hitler and his troops.

"That's my boy," he'd say to Aleksy's mother. "He's got the right idea. He'll grow up to be a strong Polish warrior after all, despite all your stupid coddling."

Still, this fourteen-year-old was no different than any other young Pole. The blood of patriotism that ran through his veins for his beloved Poland was simply expected among his people. It wasn't something one could ignore when it had been ingrained in him all his life. So, Aleksander Rostek's blood would soon prove that the same DNA pulsated through his young veins as well.

The day the Nazis arrived was not a total surprise to the little village that bordered Germany. As Hitler's troops marched across Europe in its quest to conquer the world, there had already been talk of pending war. Aleksy often heard the adults speculating over what was to come.

By 1938, not only had Hitler's troops claimed the Rhineland, but they arrogantly moved as a giant locust into Austria, eating up the rights and the land of her people and then made their way into western Czechoslovakia, promising an end to the aggression. However, a year later, eastern Czechoslovakians fell prey to the gigantic locust as it continued to ruthlessly chomp its way through Europe. Aleksy's homeland just happened to be next on Hitler's destructive path.

Even before the bombs began to fall with lightning speed, much to his father's pride, the boy had already been serving as a messenger for the City Defense Organization under the direction and supervision of his Boy Scout unit. He responsibly reported observations made to the air raid warden. This included suspicious looking planes, fires that erupted from falling bombs and buildings in which people might need assistance to evacuate.

Young Aleksy and his fellow troop members weren't home when the Nazis arrived on foot. Camping on the eastern outskirts of the city, the Boy Scouts' training session was interrupted by the distinct sound of machine guns coming from the direction of city hall. Aleksy's best friend, Koby, and another boy were ordered to bike to the city to find out what was going on there; the report was not good. They furiously pedaled back to the campsite, sliding their bike tires into an abrupt halt, sending dust in every direction.

"The Germans are at city hall," Koby reported between gasping breaths, " and they've shot our policemen and even some civilians who happened to be there!" It was obvious to Aleksy that his friend was panicked.

A local cavalry unit quickly arrived and ordered the scouts to evacuate the camp immediately. To Aleksy's dismay, the boys were instructed to continue on with this unit of burly men - no chance of returning home as danger was imminent. They were told that if the Germans caught them, they would be shot on sight. It didn't matter that they were just boys. Aleksy cringed as his eyes locked on Koby. Koby stared back before Aleksy broke the spell with a lopsided grin. "Looks like we get to play soldier for real. Arm yourself comrade!"

Aleksy could tell his friend was trying to be brave. "Yep," he replied. "Who would have ever thought that joining the Boy Scouts would require real weapons and ammo?"

"Remember when we joined up Aleksy? We were told we'd become part of the Polish army if war broke out. We just didn't think it would happen."

"Hmph," Aleksy replied as he started grabbing things they might need. "I think my old man was hoping it would come to this. He helped run the Nazis off just a year and a half ago. Now, he seems to have a thirst for either war or blood; I'm not sure which."

"He'll be plenty proud when he gets word of this, then," replied Koby.

"Hurry up!" barked a commanding officer.

The boys grabbed their backpacks and fell in step with the cavalry as if they'd been doing it for years. A rush surged through their young bodies; real life had met up with youth. Attempting fearlessness, the friends marched beside one another, ready to prove their patriotism. Forcefully grinning from ear to ear, neither dared to admit the quaking inside their boots or the sick feeling at the pit of their guts.

The local cavalry, known as the "lancers," were steeped in the tradition and times of Napoleon's own regiments. Outfitted with the modern weaponry of the day, could also carry a lance or sabre if so desired; the boys looked upon them in awe. Such a weapon spoke of the adventures of the heroes of child's play. Koby nudged his friend. "Hey, Aleksy! Perhaps we are now part of Juro Janosik's adventures! Maybe we will rob from the rich and give to the poor. Do you think we might even take home a magic arrow?"

Aleksy smiled as he marched. He knew this was Koby's childish way of dealing with the terror that had engulfed them. And regardless of what was ahead, he feared for his somewhat fragile friend.

The boys marched beside the cavalry with innocent and artificial pride as they moved toward the Polish Defense Line on the Warta River. Meanwhile, the German Air Force flew overhead with a deadly display of bombers dropping their ammo on anything in sight. Innocent civilians became targets while moving along the crowded roadways seeking refuge; such was the ugliness of war.

The cavalry unit was ordered to take the young scouts, thirty in all, under wing as they journeyed on foot toward Warsaw where the boys would report to that city's Boy Scout command. One could see the look on the soldiers' faces as if to say, "Why are we bringing children with us? They should be home with their mothers." But a command was a command and therefore, the men marched on watching as children were forced to become adults well before their time.

Cavalry and scouts alike surveyed the sunny yet blackened skies; the thunder of bombers roared in their ears, and they periodically dodged for cover as they heard the whistle of falling bombs then regrouped and marched on.

Prior to the German attack, an unsettling event had occurred before the boys had even set foot on this unexpected journey. German troops dressed as Polish soldiers staged a so-called Polish attack against a German radio station located in Gleiwitz, Germany. The intent was to justify Germany's aggression toward the people of Poland by making it appear that the Polish had taken over the broadcast station. An unfortunate man of Silesian descent, who had been taken prisoner by the Germans because he felt sorry for Poland, was dressed in a Polish uniform, shot, then left at the scene as evidence of a Polish attack.

Aleksy's father had kept him abreast of what was happening in the world; his son would not be ignorant when it came to politics.

"Those dirty Germans!" he exclaimed after reading the account aloud to his son. How dare they wear the uniform of the Polish and blame us for such an atrocity! They will rot in Hell for this, and it will still be too good of a punishment. Do you understand how important it is that the Germans pay for this filthy act, Aleksy?"

"Yes, sir," replied his wide-eyed son.

"Never forget what low-down scum they are! And when the time comes, do all you can to retaliate. You're a patriot, Boy, and it's up to you to keep this land free of anybody who tries to take our freedom away. Stand strong in the face of the enemy because if you don't, they'll kick *you* in the face and tramp all over you. Be wise, Son, and use every ounce of luck that comes your way."

"Yes, sir, Father. I'll do my best."

"Do better than your best, Boy. Make your old man proud."

This theatrical "attack" had served to incite German opinion against the Polish, thereby, turning the wheels of war toward what would now become WWII with the hope that Poland would be seen as the culprit. Faced with a monster enemy and little to no help from earlier promises by the United Kingdom and France, the patriotic passion and pride of the Polish was sparked. It was in this spirit that the faithful friends marched on.

"How much further?" asked a tired Koby after several days of endless marching, dodging missiles and sleeping in fields.

"I don't know," replied the equally tired Aleksy. "Perhaps two more according to the commander, maybe three."

"I'd give anything right now for a plate of Lucja's cabbage and sausages."

"You told me your sister can't cook."

"No, she can't, but I'd swallow it whole if I came upon it."

Aleksy chuckled, "Then you *have* gotten pretty desperate, Koby."

"One would have to be desperate to eat *her* cooking," came his sheepish reply.

Aleksy laughed. "In that case I'd probably join you in your meal; I have never felt so hungry.

What I wouldn't give for a bowl of stew stocked with meat and potatoes."

"Or meatballs with tomato sauce."

"And a slice of warm apple cake…"

"Aleksy, we must stop! My stomach growls so loud the Nazis can hear it."

"Agreed, my friend. All we're doing is teasing our stomachs, and it's sheer torture, but what I'd give just to know food awaits us at the other end."

With that, both boys picked up their steps, pressing toward an unseen but possible plate of food.

The nightly foot journey continued through forest and field as the boys obediently moved forward. Surrounded by the sight and odor of burning cities, they stayed the course and valiantly trudged on. Had they retreated, they would find no comforts of hearth and home in their once beloved village, nor for that matter, in the entire Motherland. As the Nazis rampaged the city, its citizens were either murdered or pushed into Central Poland. Included were Aleksy's mother and father and Koby's parents and siblings, as well. Little did they realize that Poland had now become the official starting place of WWII; Warsaw would lay claim to the exact historical location.

The long hike toward the Polish defense line took the troops eastward. The security along the Warta River had been broken and the scouts soon found themselves quickly retreating away from Warsaw rather than toward it. Although the Polish military had planned for a possible invasion from the Germans, they weren't prepared for the persistent bombing nor for the speed at which Hitler's forces would move against their own brave men. And just what *had* become of the promises made by their allies? The long stretch of the border proved to be too much to defend without aid. And by October the red and white flag of Poland would give way to the black and white flag of Nazi Germany, but for now Poland marched on.

Because of a special alliance pact, both Germany and Russia pledged to refrain from warfare against one another and to secretly invade a number of European countries, including Poland. This meant Aleksy and his comrades would go into battle facing the vicious Germans head-on with the brutal Russians sneaking up from behind. It was in this frightening setting that the boys faced the horrid realities of war.

As they marched, a young comrade by the name of Dominik screamed out at the sound of a nearby explosion. Koby and Aleksy, shrieked and dove their faces into the dirt at the sight of shrapnel falling all around. Arms went over heads; both men and boys lay still as the sonic blast echoed in their ears followed by an eerie calm. One by one, the boys pulled themselves up from the hard ground and surveyed the damage. Flung to the side of the road were the remains of Dominik, their childhood friend.

"Koby, Koby!" yelled Aleksy. "We need to help Dominik!"

Koby stood up and ran toward his friend; together they surveyed the remains of his shredded body then quickly fell on the ground to his side. The two boys desperately tried to put Dominik's spilled insides back where they belonged. Others joined them in their endeavor as they stuffed his intestines and other unknown parts back into the cavity of what used to be the boy's stomach. Their hands were covered in blood, as well as their faces, in an attempt to brush the hair out of their eyes and wipe away sudden tears that streamed down their faces.

Finally, the commanding officer approached them. "Time to go boys," he said.

"No, we can't go!" screamed Koby. "Dominick needs us!"

"That's an order, Soldier," came the sharp reply.

"But I'm *not* a soldier, and I never wanted to be," he blubbered through his tears. "I'm just a kid, and I want to go home!"

Aleksy helped his shaking friend rise from the ground. "It's ok, Koby. Everything will be all right once we get to Warsaw. They'll probably send us back home from there, anyway. Come on, let's just humor the commander and pretend we're soldiers a little while longer. I need you to play along, Buddy, just like we used to do. OK?"

Koby raked his sleeve beneath his nose and sniffed loudly while nodding. "We need to bury him, first, though," he said quietly.

Aleksy shook his head "no" and pulled his friend away. Still, Koby stopped and removed his own jacket, respectfully covering their friend. He then gulped air and sobbed.

Aleksy put his arm around Koby and helped him rejoin the column of marchers which had already started to move forward. Koby cried unashamedly in the arms of his friend. The other boys looked solemn but said nothing, internalizing the events they had just witnessed.

It was a hard pill to swallow, especially when Aleksy, nor the other boys, had the luxury of mourning their loss. This was war, and there was no time for grief or remembrance. So, dumping their shock and sadness onto the body of their dead friend and classmate, they moved on with no time to spare for liturgies. A day would eventually come for thinking and reflecting, but for now, they were patriots of Poland headed to Warsaw to avenge the enemy—the devil himself.

As Aleksy and Koby continued to march, their eyes spoke what their voices could not: heartbreak, fear, anger, confusion. Koby swiped at his face again; Aleksy turned his head to give him a bit of privacy. The terror of losing Dominick had served to confirm that they were now soldier men. And soldier men didn't cry.

Traveling mostly at night and sleeping in the woods, the troops finally reached the capital city on September 8, only one week since commencing their journey. Once there, these impressionable teenagers were amazed to find anywhere between 1,000 to 1,500 scouts in uniform, serving not as boy scouts, but as young soldiers.

The boys were immediately assigned in pairs to military support positions. Aleksy and Mieszko, a Polish scout from Warsaw, carried both food and water to machine gunners operating on the outskirts of the city while Koby and another boy loaded sandbags onto a truck. A damp cellar of a bombed out apartment building served as the gunners' bunker while the company kitchen and ammunition dump were located several miles from the boys' post. As the bombs fell, Aleksy and Mieszko hastened along their deadly route, twice a day, enabling the gunners to solidly hold their positions. They carried soup in kettles with covers to the tired and famished soldiers. While no bread substantiated the meal, it didn't matter. The men were simply glad to receive what food they could along with the ammunition boxes, one more sustenance of life while death flowed around them.

One morning, as the boys dodged bullets and schrapnel, Aleksy tripped over his own boot laces falling into the dirt and grime. The precious liquid he carried seeped into the earth while he fumbled to recover the loose vegetables that piled at his feet. Mieszko quickly set his kettle to the side to help his friend retrieve the disappearing treasure. Aleksy cried out when he looked into the half-empty kettle. But there was nothing to be done except carry on.

The soldiers were quick to welcome the boys, knowing they brought food. The commander pulled the lid from Aleksy's kettle and looked inside in disbelief. Yanking the kettle from Mieszko's hands, he wrenched off the lid looking a bit relieved.

"What happened?" he asked.

Aleksy dropped his head in shame and explained how in his haste he had tripped over his own boot laces. The commanding officer grimaced.

"I'm sorry, but there's barely enough for the men as it is. You two will forgo lunch today and perhaps be more careful next time."

"Yes sir," the boys responded, saluting and turning to leave.

As they made their way back, Aleksy could hear the growling of his comrade's empty stomach. He would have preferred a punch to the face.

Mieszko simply shrugged. "It could have been worse; you could have lost the whole pot."

Aleksy sighed with relief knowing at supper he would give his friend a larger portion from his own. Meanwhile, they would dream of the taste of potato dumplings like their mothers used to cook.

In spite of the strength and determination of soldiers and scouts alike, the power of the Nazis proved to be even greater. In September, all troops stationed in the outlying areas of the city, were ordered to return to Warsaw. The young Aleksy and his comrades found conditions there deplorable as the city streets were overflowing with the dead, both soldiers and civilians. It would have been the Scouts' job to assist the military and the Red Cross. However, any aid that could have been provided to the Red Cross was now lost among bombs and bullets as there had been no time to turn away from assisting soldiers caught in the thick of battle. The Red Cross would have to wait.

In spite of its tireless defense, much to the Boy Scouts' horror, Warsaw surrendered to the evil power of the Nazis on September 27, 1939. The "secret" partnership of the Nazis and Soviets was coming to light. Caught in the midst of it were a multitude of young boys wearing the Boy Scout insignia. Boys like Aleksy and Koby who loved life, their family and friends. Boys who sought the adventure of summer days and camping in the woods. Boys whose only hope now lay in the hands of God. They had become homeless children without an identity, nothing more than war orphans. Being a soldier was proving more daunting than either Aleksy or Koby had ever imagined. So much for boyhood games. Juro Janosik could keep his magic arrows and his supernatural powers for all they cared. He could travel about the countryside robbing from the rich to give to the poor. Aleksy and Koby just wanted to go home.

Chapter 2
The Price of War

Elise Cornell tossed the newspaper aside from her position on the floor. "All that's in this crazy thing is politics! I'm so tired of hearing about war and Hitler. I'd rather read about fashions, Aunt Emma."

The middle-aged woman smiled as she continued to darn her husband's sock.

"I know, Elise, but the important thing is that you continue to practice your English."

"I do – everyday at school whether I want to or not!"

Emma laughed. "And I guess that's not to your liking either."

"Of course not! Science and history are so boring. Why don't they offer a class on fashion – like what's new in Paris? Or the latest movie stars? I wouldn't mind reading about those kind of things, at least they're useful."

"I would have thought the same thing at your age," replied the girl's smiling aunt. "As a matter-of-fact, I wouldn't mind flipping through a new fashion magazine even now. I did see the latest copy of *Good Housekeeping* in Carter's Drug Store the other day and picked it up ……"

Elise's facial expression took on a look of hope then dropped as her aunt continued.

"…. but decided I really didn't need it after all….so, I got this instead."

Elise squealed when her aunt pulled the latest copy of *Glamour* magazine from her bright yellow sewing basket. Jumping up, the girl threw her arms around her aunt. She was the best American aunt a girl could have!

"Well," declared her aunt returning the hug, "I see it doesn't take much to win *you* over."

Elise let go of her Aunt Emma and curled up on the sofa to peruse the new magazine while the older lady put away her sewing and stood up. "I guess I'd better get started on supper. Your Uncle Paul will be home soon, and he'll be hungrier than a bear."

"Need some help?" asked Elise, hoping she would say no.

"And take you away from all those fashions? Are you kidding?" laughed her aunt as she headed toward the kitchen. "No, thanks. I'd rather deal with a hungry bear."

The teenager smiled, thinking how blessed she was to have such a wonderful life; she knew it wouldn't be the same for her in France right now. Still, she greatly missed her mother and father as well as her grandmother.

Elise's mind slipped back to the memory of her parents' decision to send her to New York. She'd been startled when she learned she'd be going to the states to sit out the war with her father's brother and sister-in-law. She had clung to her parents begging them not to "make" her leave her family and all she'd ever known. Still, they had firmly pried her fingers lose explaining that now that Hitler had invaded France, they needed to keep her safe.

"But Maman, I can't go across the sea all alone. What if a big storm comes up, and we're ship wrecked? Or what if I don't know where to go when I reach New York? I could get lost in a foreign city! You would never see me again!"

Elise's father gently led her to the floral divan and motioned for her to sit down. "Elise," he said in his North American accent, "you are everything to us, and we could not bear to lose you. But seeing what happened to Simone…"

"Her *mother* was killed, too," cried out the girl. "So, why won't you and Maman go with me to America?"

"You know the reasons we can't go. My service with the French Foreign Legion is expected, and besides, it's a matter of integrity to fight next to my American brothers. As for your mother, she can't leave your grand-mère because she is too sick and too old to make such a trip. I shouldn't have to explain all of this, Elise."

"But I may never see grand-mère again once I leave France."

Elise's parents looked at one another unsure what to say.

"Yes, Elise," softly agreed her mother. "There is a good chance you will never see her again. That's why you must spend as much time as possible with your grandmother before the ship departs. That would make her very happy, don't you think?"

The girl wiped her tears against the fabric of her sweater. "When does the ship leave?" she asked in a halting voice.

"In two weeks," said her father. "But your grandmother doesn't know that yet."

"Two weeks!" exclaimed the thirteen-year-old as she glared at her father. "First, you didn't even ask my opinion on the matter and then, you didn't allow any time for me to adjust to the idea! Not to mention that I won't even have the time to properly tell my friends goodbye! How could you?"

"Elise," came her father's stern reply. "You do not speak to your mother and me in that tone. You've been taught better."

"I'm sorry Papa, but I'm in such shock, and it's all happening so fast!"

"We realize that, Kitten, but we must get you to safety while we can. France is in great danger, and I can't allow any harm to come to you."

"But Maman and Grand- mère…"

"We've already been through that, Elise. You'll be leaving for America in two weeks. So, start packing and saying your goodbyes."

"I want to see Grand-mère," responded Elise tearfully.

Her parents watched her sulk toward the front door with slumped shoulders, their own hearts breaking with their decision.

"Couldn't you have been a little kinder, Edward?" asked his wife.

The man sighed. "There is no kindness when it comes to war, ma chérie."

Edward Cornell knew what it was to say good-bye to family and to adjust to a new culture. But in his case, all because he'd fallen in love. At least he'd made the choice himself.

"I hate this war," whispered his wife. "All it does is bring agony and sorrow – especially to the lives of children."

Her husband hugged her and kissed the top of her head. "Yes, Maman, it is always the children who pay, and if I can protect our only child from being forced into early adulthood or even an early death, I intend to do so."

The girl's mother shuddered as she thought about Elise's best friend, Simone - her young life cut short because of one man's selfish act. She hated Hitler with an unhealthy passion, and she hated all that he was doing throughout Europe, especially when it came to ripping families apart either by death or physical separation. Sighing, she leaned into her husband's embrace, mentally noting that she'd need to make confession at mass and to light a candle for the most vulnerable of all victims of war – the innocent children.

Chapter 3

A Boy Scout Prisoner of War

On the day of surrender, all Boy Scouts were ordered to report to the Warsaw soccer field. Although the Germans had not yet arrived to take charge, the scouts were commanded to stay on the field overnight. They were tired, dirty, and hungry; adjectives befitting those who have just experienced battle, as well as those deemed orphans. And sleeping on the hard earth without the benefit of a blanket wasn't too appealing. Yet even in their state of despair, sleep did come for most as it eventually does to exhausted bodies and minds.

"Aleksy, are you awake?" whispered Koby.

Aleksy grunted to indicate he was.

"What do you think? Could we make a run for it?"

Aleksy's eyes roamed the field, the moonlight revealing the impossible. "If you're ready to die."

Guards stood laughing and talking in hushed tones. Some stood or sat on wooden bleachers while others hovered around the perimeters of the field, ever watchful. Guns were held in the ready. Aside from the well-manned spectator bleachers, there was little to no covering. The moon would only serve as an additional search light to those already established.

Aleksy shook his head. Koby sure could be dumb for such a smart friend. His A+ average didn't hold water when it came to common sense. Aleksy, on the other hand, he was smart; his smarts didn't necessarily come from books, though. He took pride in his ability to figure things out – common sense is what he had. He'd stack that against Koby's book smarts any day. Escape? Not a chance. At least not now. If he had a book, he'd smack his buddy over the head.

"Go to sleep, Koby," he said.

"I wish I could but…Aleksy?"

"Yeah?"

"Are you ever afraid?"

"Sometimes."

"But I mean like right now."

"Maybe a little."

"Are you afraid of dying?"

Aleksy pondered the thought a moment. "Not really, because I don't think that's going to happen."

"Ever?"

"Sure, one day. But we'll be old men then."

"Dominik wasn't old," replied Koby. "He was just a kid like us."

"That was Dominik, Koby. It was just his time."

"What if it's our time?"

"Then, we'll go like Dominik – like a good soldier."

"Do you think even good soldiers can die afraid?"

"Nope, because they die as proud patriots, and there must be special rewards for them."

"Like what?"

"Maybe no time in purgatory, just straight to Heaven."

"Why aren't you afraid, Aleksy?"

"Because I'm a lucky person, and I don't intend to die anytime soon."

"Oh," responded Koby as he tried to absorb this information. "So, Dominik wasn't lucky?"

"It was just his time, Koby. Go to sleep. If it'll make you feel better, you can light a candle for him when you get home."

"OK. Goodnight." Koby turned onto his side, and a few minutes later, Aleksy heard the even breathing of his friend.

Afraid? It was a luxury in which he couldn't indulge – not if he was to survive.

Early the next morning, the official announcement was made: Warsaw had surrendered, a fact confirmed by the now descending uniforms of the enemy. The Scout Commander had been ordered to gather all the Polish Boy Scouts as the Germans would soon arrive. Only half of the original group of boys from Aleksy's village had survived to this point.

The day was spent unlike any other on a soccer field as the jovial cheers of the usual soccer fans were now only those offered by the ghosts of memory. The game had been played, the victors declared winners although their offensive aggression had been somewhat lacking in sportsmanship. Divided into two teams, the Germans and the Poles, one would lord the upper hand over the other, regardless of what the referee might think. After all, there were no fair rules to this game, not on this day, not on this field. A field for children, yet a field of war.

When the Germans arrived in the afternoon, they announced to the Boy Scouts of Warsaw and its surrounding vicinities to return home and get rid of their Scout uniforms. If they were ever seen in them again, it would mean certain death.

The boys of Aleksy's village braced themselves for the same words of departure, however, this wasn't to be the case. They silently studied the two Nazis in their black uniforms as they approached the group of young men still wearing the skins of children. They watched the soldiers expectantly, waiting to be released to their mothers and fathers. Aleksy and his comrades anticipated the speech and were more than ready to hand over their own Scout uniforms. The two soldiers spoke perfect Polish, and the boys listened intently as instructions were delivered.

"As you have already seen and heard," stated one of the German soldiers, "our Fuhrer has taken over Poland to expand his German empire. You have come from afar, and your locality is well underway to becoming part of the German Third Reich, so we have no need for you to return."

"All Poles," continued the second man, "are being removed from that area. This means your families are being pushed out of your villages to make their way to Central Poland, or they are already dead."

"As for you boys," said the first soldier, "you are now war orphans. As you have nowhere to go, you will be taken into Germany." The shock of his orders sent electrical currents reverberating throughout the group of unsuspecting boys.

Koby turned toward Aleksy and whispered beneath his breath, "But you said we'd get to go home once we reached Warsaw. The others got to leave."

Aleksy lowered his head and whispered so as not to be heard, "It looks like there's been a change of plans, my friend. Just do as they say, and it will humor them."

"But I want to go home."

"Who's talking?" bellowed a nearby German soldier.

No one breathed nor moved. They may have been children, but to the Nazis, they were still the enemy. The over-bearing soldier walked around and between the boys as they all huddled in their group. He appeared to enjoy intimidating them.

"I suggest you not talk when the Fuhrer's men are giving you instructions. It is disrespectful to our leader."

The boys stared at the ground until the moment had passed and the German soldier had sauntered away as if he were Hitler himself.

Aleksy pushed his apprehension aside. He knew from that moment on he would begin his long journey back to freedom. He just didn't know how long it would take or what it would involve. And little did he know that he was already being watched closely. Still, he fully believed the Nazis would not be a match to his innate will to survive.

The boys were loaded onto two army trucks and taken into Germany. It was a trip that took one and a half physical days, but mentally, a lifetime and a half. Upon arrival, Aleksy and his comrades were then taken to military barracks where they were fed and locked into a large room. Their final demands for the night: "Go to sleep," orders defied by all until exhaustion took over.

Early the next morning, they were awakened and once again fed, uncertain of their future until they found themselves face to face with a room full of burly German farmers. The two Polish speaking soldiers reappeared to inform the teens that each would be assigned to a farmer to help him in his labors. If the Scouts tried to contact one another or attempted an escape, it would result in death; they would be shot immediately.

Aleksy, along with Koby and some of the other boys, contemplated their fate. So hopeless was the order some even cried, but the guards frowned harshly, and the tears stopped for fear of being shot even then.

Later that afternoon, Aleksy was called out by a uniformed German and presented to a "fat man" dressed in bib overalls and a tattered work shirt. He was told that the man had a farm in a village located next to the Baltic Sea where Aleksy would assist him. Paperwork laying claim to the young prisoner was then shuffled about between the farmer and the satisfied Nazi. Before leaving, Aleksy bid a final farewell to his remaining childhood friends, most of whom he would never see again. He solemnly shook hands with those closest to him, but when he stood face to face with Koby, the boy grabbed hold of Aleksy and hugged his neck. He sniffed and tried to control himself.

"Aleksy, what will we do?" he whimpered. "How will we ever get home? I'm scared! I want to go home!"

A German soldier clamped his hand on Koby's shoulder and pulled him away from his friend. "Shut-up, you cry baby!" And then turning to his comrades, "Perhaps we could find a pacifier for this one," he snickered.

Aleksy saluted his friend and quickly mumbled, "Stay strong, Koby. It is our survival." Yet he could feel the sting of tears rising in his own eyes as he tucked his head to avoid humiliation.

Aleksander Rostek soon found himself on one of two trucks bound for his new "home." A young German soldier acting as guard, rode with him amid a host of furniture and other household items, no doubt stolen from the dwellings of Polish officers. As the two jostled along in silence, the trip seemed endless. And although it would be awhile before Aleksy could speak German, he decided it was time to at least attempt a conversation. After all, his sanity was at stake.

"So, where are you from?" he asked casually.

What shock when the man answered, "Berlin."

"So, you understand Polish?"

"Better than I speak it."

Aleksy nodded. “Do you know where they’re taking me?”

“Near the Baltic Sea.”

“So, what’s it like there, the farmer’s property?”

“I have no idea, but I hear the farmer you’ll live with is somewhat strict. Still, he’s known to be fair with his prisoners and his hired help.”

Aleksy was surprised. “There are other prisoners?”

The soldier shrugged. “I guess there are at times, but I don’t know about now.”

“Do you think he’ll release me soon?”

“I doubt it; there is a war on. You ask too many questions.”

He grinned at the German. “And for what reason is there a war? All I have seen is your great Fuhrer rolling into other countries and taking what’s not his.”

“But that’s where you’re wrong, Pole. He’s reclaiming the Fatherland’s empire and simply restoring what belonged to him to start with.”

Aleksy shrugged, “Fatherland, Motherland, who cares? He’s ruthless and takes advantage of people through the use of fear to get what he wants.”

Aleksy had overstepped the boundaries with his comments. He could tell by the dirty look the German was giving him.

“I suggest we end this conversation now,” said the soldier. “ I cannot sit by and allow you to attack our great leader.”

Aleksy shrugged but did not reply. The guard could think what he wanted, but the Polish boy knew the truth of it.

“There *are* ways we can keep an eye on you, Pole. So, don’t try anything you’ll regret. If you are good to us, Hitler’s regime will be good to you.”

Aleksy snickered; he couldn’t help it, but quickly received a hard blow to his jawline in return.

“Point taken,” he said as he stared down the guard while rubbing his sore jaw before retreating into silence. When the caravan of two reached the midway point of its destination, the Polish boy was fed his supper then locked into a police holding cell, enabling his fat overseer a worry-free night of rest.

Early the next morning, a new German driver came to the prison to pick up his captive and eventually hand him over to the care of the unkempt fat man. Aleksy was returned to the transport truck where he discovered yesterday's soldier would once again escort him. Trial and error had taught him to keep his mouth shut as the truck continued north toward the Baltic Sea. After several hours of a silent ride, they reached their final destination by noon that day - a rather small village. The boy studied his surroundings, taking in the large farmhouse and fenced farmland which would serve as his place of residence. The fat man laboriously climbed from the truck's cab to address a group of neighbors already assembled there. Aleksy strained to understand their conversation believing it focused on the war and himself.

The men looked Aleksy over, studying him as if he were some kind of scientific specimen. To a fourteen-year-old, such attention wasn't so welcoming, especially when he stood before the enemy still dressed in a very dirty Boy Scout uniform.

Although uncomfortable, Aleksy did not feel fear toward his enemies at that particular moment. However, he quickly developed a strong dislike for Lars, the brother-in-law of his new "master." Along with his Hitler Youth uniform, Lars wore his pride and zeal on his shoulders for all to see, as well as an obvious disgust and disdain for the Polish boy standing before him. Aleksy knew the Hitler-Jugend attire represented blind obedience to a monster who controlled many a young boy as if he were a puppet on a string. And just like the mesmerized youth of Hitler's army, Aleksy could do nothing but obey as he later followed his jail warden to his assigned quarters.

The warden, however, proved to be one of a gentler nature as his "host" was a young female. She took Aleksy by the hand and pointing to herself, told him her name was "Romana." He would soon learn that she served as the household maid.

Ramana led the teenage boy to a small room attached to the back of the large house, speaking consistently in her German tongue as she pulled him along. Perhaps she spoke words of comfort telling him not to be afraid. Regardless, Aleksy never understood a single word she spoke.

His new home consisted of a bed and one small chair accessorized by an even smaller barred window, lest he forget this was not a country vacation. As Romana departed, Aleksy heard the distinctive sound of the door being locked.

Since there was nothing to do or even see from the small window, he paced the floor a while then lay down and studied the ceiling. He couldn't help but wonder what things were like for the friends to whom he had bid farewell only the day before. He especially worried about Koby and how his friend was faring or if he'd been shot already because of so much crying. It was a side of his friend he'd never seen before. Although Aleksy knew Koby was somewhat frail, his recent emotional reactions had completely unnerved him. He would do his best to locate his friend as soon as he returned to Poland. Not returning wasn't even an option; he best start planning his escape.

The boy stood up and walked back to the small window where he tried to pull the metal bars inward, but it was no use. He studied how they were cemented into the window-well and scratched his head. He would definitely need something he could use to file the bars down, but where in the world would he find such a thing? Ah! Perhaps Romana could help. He would begin working on his friendship with her right away. Meanwhile, he was stuck with no tools, no comic books, no paper, no pencil and no food. For now, he'd simply have to make the best of it. At least he could sleep, and on the in-between, mentally work on his escape plan.

Somehow the past twenty-four hours had seemed like an eternity rather than a day. He wondered how long he would be held here and if anyone in the world even had a clue where he was or for that matter, if anyone even cared. But of course his parents cared, didn't they? Even his father, with his harsh ways, had to care a little. After all, he now had a son of which he could be proud, a soldier son, even if he was only a prisoner of war.

Aleksy sighed and turned over on the small bed. Rather than feeling fear he simply felt bored and yes, trapped. As his mind focused on the war, he knew the Polish were in anguish over the loss of their country. Add to that the Germans' barbaric treatment toward the civilians of Poland. Both young and old simply embodied an object of hatred in the minds and hearts of the Nazis. Aleksy stared at the ceiling thinking how useless war is.

His reverie was finally brought to an end when he heard the key turn in the lock once more. Romana had returned with an armload of civilian clothes and left with Aleksy's Boy Scout uniform. Once again, alone with his thoughts, he lay on the bed until early evening when the serving maid reappeared. The familiar click of the keys caused Aleksy's brain to churn. Forget the hard work of filing through metal bars; it would be a lot easier just to obtain the key.

This time the maid took her captive to the kitchen where they both ate supper on common ground - she no better than a prisoner, and he no better than a serving maid. People who lived for the German Reich had greater matters with which to deal than the feeding of a farm hand. After all, the landowner himself was a declared Nazi, and his die-hard wife even refused to look at the prisoner. Her own brother, Lars, was the leader of the village "Hitler-Jugend", and to him, this Polish Boy Scout was lower than a worm, the defeated enemy and nothing more. Yet time would prove that Aleksy Rostek was indeed so much more.

As he quietly sat chewing his German cuisine, he had the strange feeling someone was watching his every move. He looked uncomfortably about the room before refocusing his attention on Romana who smiled and coaxed him to eat more. Yes, he was a prisoner of the mighty German Reich which meant even the walls watched – and reported all they saw.

Chapter 4
From Polish Patriot to "Hitler-Jungend"

To the young Lars, Hitler was master of all, and he hated everybody who did not like Hitler. This feeling of hatred was obvious toward Aleksy.

As Aleksy had now been assigned to cleaning the horse stalls and other jobs around the barn, he ran into Lars on occasion. Lars would look at him with disgust and then bark orders in German that Aleksy couldn't understand although he tried.

One day, while cleaning the stalls, Aleksy had turned to leave when he came face to face with the Hitler Youth. Lars blocked his way. Whenever Aleksy stepped to the left to go around him, Lars stepped to the right and whenever the boy stepped to the right, Lars stepped to the left, arms folded, eyes hard. It was a game of cat and mouse that played out only when the owner of the farm appeared and blasted the German boy in a loud voice. The Hitler worshipper spat on the ground then walked away.

Aleksy gave the farmer a smile of gratitude and a nod to which the farmer responded with an angry look before moving on. It was as if the prisoner had instigated it all.

"Humph," thought Aleksy, "nobody likes me except the farmer's hunting dogs. At least *they* seem to feel sorry for me." He welcomed their companionship although they smelled like a barnyard. Still, it was better than having no one to talk to, and their wagging tails did make him smile.

Aleksy soon found that he had Sundays free from his farm labors. Since he could not go beyond the fenced farmland, he took to spending those afternoons with the dogs he'd befriended, teaching them new tricks. These four-legged companions were his only ticket to normalcy in his prison induced world, for even the neighboring children gave him odd looks. As they passed by the farm's fence, they watched and gawked as if they were at the local zoo.

At least Romana tried to be nice to him. Whenever she took him to the kitchen she would try to teach him her language. She would point to items and say the German word. "Der Stuhl," she said pointing to the wooden chair on which he sat. "Der stuhl," Aleksy repeated patting the chair.

"Gute," she would say smiling then move to the next item.

"Tisch."

"Tisch," responded Aleksy tapping on the table.

This continued for days with Romana quizzing the boy and affirming his progress. They would take turns switching between Polish and German, pointing out various objects in the kitchen. During his tutoring sessions, Aleksy was watchful for the key that unlocked the door to his prison. He was beginning to feel like a Polish spy and took great pride in his courage. His eyes would scan the room looking for a nail on which the key hung, but a nail was nowhere to be found. Then suddenly one day, he saw the girl pull the key from her apron pocket as she returned him to his quarters. Aleksy smacked himself upside the head. Why hadn't he thought of that, he wondered.

The next day, he was ready as he pointed toward her apron.

" Schürze," she said smiling.

"Schürze," he replied.

He then mimicked putting the apron on to which a laughing Romana untied the pink strings, pulled it over her head, then handed it to him. Aleksy laughingly tied the frilly apparel around his own neck then proceeded to waltz Romana around the room before pulling the key from his pocket and indicating how to say it in German.

"Schlüsse," came a clearly male voice from behind. Aleksy turned to see Lars glaring at him just before jerking the key from the prisoner's hand. Romana began to tremble and took a step back. It didn't stop Lars from stepping up to the girl and slapping her fully in the face. Prisoner or not, Aleksy had to stand up for his female friend. His fist flew into the smug smile of the junior

Nazi standing before him. "How dare you hit a woman," he screamed as he jumped on the man's back and proceeded to pulverize him.

Lars ducked his head and jerked back and forth trying to rid himself of the Polish man now attached to him. Romana simply cowered in the corner of the kitchen wringing a dishcloth in her hands while tears poured down her face.

As the two young men now danced around the kitchen they slammed into the cupboard knocking over glass dishes and food supplies. Pictures fell from the walls and the glass window rattled.

"Stoppen!" suddenly yelled a loud voice. Aleksy and Lars came to a sudden halt to find the farmer and his wife glaring at Aleksy. Lar's sister ran to her brother's side and cooed over his wounds, petting him like he was a little rabbit.

The farmer grabbed Aleksy by the arm and dragged him to his "prison cell" to await execution for all he knew. He slammed the door shut then called to Lars for the missing key who quickly showed up and locked the Polish boy inside. Aleksy cringed at the sound of the click; that was the last time he'd ever see that key.

He wasn't sure how many days passed before he was finally allowed to work in the barn again. But one thing he did know was Romana was nowhere to be seen. His food was now delivered to him through the bars of the small window; he was no longer taken to the kitchen. And no doubt, to add injury to Lars' behavior as well, *he* was now the one who served the meal, if one could call it a meal. Three times a day he now received one hard *Brotchen* roll. Biting into the tough crust was enough of a challenge, but the endless chewing caused his jaw to hurt. He depended on the quart jar of well water to wash it down. Otherwise, it stuck in his throat. But lucky for him, the water was cool.

As the days continued to pass, Aleksy exercised in his room, knowing he would need to keep fit because, when his opportunity to escape did come, he wanted to have enough strength to run, jump, push, tug, whatever his escape would require of him. He also spent time reviewing in his mind all the German words he had learned from Romana, wondering what had become of her. He knew he was the reason for her sudden disappearance which made him feel a little sad. At least like the dogs, she had been kind to him.

Eventually, autumn turned into winter. The last month of the year proved to be cruel and cold to a boy who had no warm clothes and had to spend Sunday afternoons in an unheated room. Yet in spite of his dismal situation, a glimmer of hope had been sparked. The fat farmer was finally allowing Aleksy to return to his work assignment as he obviously needed his help, and the farmer's German miller had managed to convey that seven Polish prisoners of war would be arriving soon after Christmas. Aleksy was delighted as now he would have someone to talk to. While most Polish children were watching for the arrival of the festive Mikolaj and the gifts he would bring to all good boys and girls, Aleksy eagerly awaited the completion of an additional room which would house his comrades, the best and only present he would receive that year.

True to the miller's word, the Polish prisoners of war arrived right after the holiday. They consisted of six soldiers and their sergeant, as well as a German officer who served as their guard. By now, the companion-starved Aleksy wanted desperately to converse with those of his motherland. It had been almost four months since he had had a conversation with someone in his native tongue. What joy he felt when he discovered that the German guard spoke a little Polish. He approached the man cautiously.

"I'd like to visit with the Polish soldiers, sir," he stated as best he could mixing German with Polish.

"Polish soldiers?" he asked rather amused. "No Polish soldiers here – only prisoners."

"Well, sir, they won't be working on Sundays," replied the determined teenager, "so, may I visit them then?"

The guard summoned the imprisoned sergeant and asked him to translate. Once he understood that Aleksy was a Polish youngster given to the farmer by a German military unit, he responded that the boy could indeed visit the sergeant as well as the rest of the prisoners on Sundays. Aleksy grinned. How did he ever get to be so lucky?

Aleksy quickly informed Herr Fat Man that the German officer had granted permission for Sunday visits with the Polish prisoners if the farmer was in agreement. Somewhat surprised by the guard's leniency, the man grunted his acceptance then moved on to farming matters.

A mentoring relationship soon developed between the young Boy Scout and the Polish sergeant. Using his common sense, Aleksy couldn't help but believe this friendship would lay the groundwork for eventual escape, even survival as the sergeant taught him everything he could.

"It's important that you learn to speak the German language as well as the Nazis," he said. "So, gather up as many German newspapers as you can; you'll have lessons every week."

It was a tall order but one that could prove to be of great value. So, the boy busied himself with hiding German newspapers beneath his thin mattress. While it wasn't an ideal hiding place, no one seemed to care about the belongings in his sparsely furnished room. Besides, the added papers provided another layer of warmth and cushion as he slept, not to mention extra body warmth when he slid the goods into his waistband for easy smuggling.

Also, their purpose proved to be twofold: to teach the German language to a Polish boy and to keep the Polish prisoners in touch with the outside world. Of course, the propaganda was evident from the start as headlines and articles boasted of Germany's imperialism. And although their sickening claims were a frustration through which to wade, they served as the perfect grammar book.

The local papers were full of European updates: Belgian Army Surrenders to the Germans; City of Narvik, Norway Captured by French, Polish and British Forces. The latter came as good news to the Polish POWs as it now confirmed that Poland was indeed still in the war.

The Polish sergeant was adamant that Aleksy immerse himself into the German language; he also insisted that the boy do his job at the mill and on the farm as well as he could in order to regain trust after the "key" incident in the kitchen with Romana. And he was instructed not to ever "hassle with Lars" again and to avoid any close relationships with German boys once he was given privileges to leave the farmyard. Although Aleksy felt such freedom would be long in coming, it eventually did show up in a pleasant way that spring of 1940, right after his fifteenth birthday, when Herr Fat Farmer announced that Aleksy was now free to leave the farm on Sunday afternoons. He could go to the beach or the village if he liked. Aleksy smiled knowing *he* had further destinations in mind.

One sunny day, after the farmer's announcement, Aleksy was summoned by Lars to wash six horses in the Baltic Sea. Lars would be leaving at the end of summer to join the Schutzstaffel, otherwise known as the SS or Hitler's bodyguards, and Aleksy couldn't wait for him to be gone. He despised taking orders from this egotistical Hitler clone.

As Aleksy scrubbed down the hard-working horses, the local children and teens passed by studying him with interest. No doubt, parents had warned their children to be wary of the foreign prisoner of war. He was the enemy, and they must never forget that. Yet, as the children stared at him, he continued his work, occasionally speaking a greeting until the spectators began to warm up to him.

Even with his newfound freedom, time passed slowly for Aleksy. In the long run, it proved to be beneficial, providing ample time to learn the much-needed German language. By using his God-given skill of a quick mind, Aleksy soon picked up on the spoken, as well as the written communication that may have taken others years to learn. Some might say it was a good dose of divine intervention, but not the young Aleksy who proudly believed it to be his own "smarts." By the summer of 1940, he spoke German like a native-born citizen, accent and all.

It was late summer when Aleksy found himself accepted by the German boys as if he were one of them. He was even allowed to watch their Hitler Youth drill every Saturday at the soccer field, and as a result, he and Bruno became friends.

This native German boy seemed to find much pleasure in hanging out with his new Polish friend. Whether he had plans to assist in Aleksy's escape was difficult to say, but the obvious loop holes that came about because of Bruno's interest, couldn't be ignored.

As their friendship developed, the Polish officer advised Aleksy to be careful not to discuss the war with Bruno or with Bruno's friends. "Be smart and listen," he said, "but do not get into political subjects with the boys." Then the invitation came.

Aleksy was invited to travel to a nearby city (about twenty-five miles away) with Bruno and his mother. While it may not have been the adventure that would beckon to most young men, it excited a boy who longed for a taste of freedom. The trip had been planned only to visit Bruno's uncle who had suffered war injuries. Still, Aleksy desperately wanted to go; his hunger for freedom from the farm grew into a savory morsel, and this outing would eventually become a feast to help satisfy that gnawing hunger.

But first things first. Aleksy wasn't sure if his over-seer would allow him to make the trip. He approached the man a bit timidly. "Sir, may I speak with you a moment?" he asked as the farmer tossed hay onto the back of a truck.

"I'm busy boy, what do you want?"

"My friend Bruno and his mother are taking a trip into the city to see Bruno's uncle. And they've invited me to join them."

"Is that so?" asked the German farmer wiping sweat from his forehead.

"Yes sir. We'll take the early train on Sunday and return well before dark."

The farmer studied the boy closely. "I don't know," he said. "You've been given freedom to go to the beach and other places around the village, but I'm not sure if I can trust you to go twenty-five miles by train."

Aleksy dropped his head in exaggerated disappointment. "I am very sorry, sir. I realize I lost your trust several months ago but had hoped it is now restored."

The man paused. "So, you're going to visit Bruno's uncle?"

"Yes sir, he is actually in the hospital with his war injuries."

"Ahh.....a soldier of the Third Reich. Why didn't you say so, lad?"

Aleksy shrugged, looking hopeful now.

"Yes, by all means. Go. Show respect to our great warriors. This is a good trip for you to make. Perhaps it will help you appreciate Hitler and his war machine. Ha, you might even learn how real soldiers fight."

He then handed the boy 10 marks. Although a small amount, this was the first time he'd been paid for his work.

"Thank you, sir," Aleksy said as he turned away. He didn't want to look too excited, so he forced himself to walk back to the barn at a normal pace. But once inside he was deliriously happy, knowing exposure to the train lines and to a large city would be advantageous to his escape.

Aleksy and Bruno walked to the nearby train station to purchase tickets in advance. Bruno presented his money and his ID along with that of his mother to the ticket agent. The transaction was smooth, and he soon held the important slips of paper in his hand.

Aleksy stepped to the window and requested his own ticket.

"Let me see your ID," mumbled the station master as he continued stamping documents.

"I don't have any ID," Aleksy replied.

"All people fifteen years old and older must have an ID to travel," snapped the annoyed agent as he looked up. "There is a war out there and the rules have to be obeyed. Nobody travels in this country unless he or she has a valid identity." The man turned back to his paperwork totally dismissing the boy.

Aleksy looked at his friend, not sure what to do. Did this mean he would not be leaving the village after all, even if it was only a short trip?

Bruno suggested that they go see the "Wachtmeister," the only local police. Thanking the station master, they followed the streets that led to the police department. Aleksy walked cautiously behind Bruno as they entered the small office.

The law enforcer was very kind and listened as the boys explained their dilemma. He then opened a file and pulled out a brown folder which apparently contained details on the young prisoner. The boys shifted from foot to foot as the man perused the information. Finally, he laid the official papers aside and announced that he had no authority to issue the ID. He explained that the boy would have to write to the Lebensborn office in order to obtain it as Aleksy was under the guardianship of a "Foster Parent." Aleksy gave the man a puzzled look.

"Once you were assigned to your current guardian," he explained, "you were recorded as a foster child. Under our Lebensborn Program you were immediately added to the pool of potential Aryians. In other words, because you meet the characteristics our Fuhrer considers important for his new race, blonde hair and blue-eyes among other things, you were added to their files."

Bruno grinned and slapped Aleksy on the back. "Congratulations, my friend! Sounds like you are destined to be a Polish stud!"

"A what?"

The Wachtmeister laughed loudly. "Consider it an honor, young man. You could be called up to perform the services needed to assure the pure race Adolf Hitler is working toward. Don't worry as the girls he'll pair you with will be the most beautiful blondes you can ever imagine."

Aleksy was disgusted. What kind of mind did this Hitler have? As he opened the door to leave, he thanked the still laughing German.

Once Bruno was able to get past the idea of Aleksy contributing to the new Aryian race, he returned to the seriousness of the matter at hand.

"Aleksy, we don't have time to correspond with the Lebensborn office if we're to visit the city on Sunday."

" I guess it wasn't meant for me to go after all," responded Aleksy with slumping shoulders. Just as they rounded the corner, they nearly ran into the Wachtmeister's son, Marius, who seemed somewhat surprised to see them.

"Why the long faces?" he asked.

"We just found out that Aleksy can't get a travel ID before Sunday. He was going into the city with us to visit my uncle."

"Bruno," he said with a sigh, "take Aleksy to the photo shop and get the photographer to take his picture, then bring it straight to me after you pick it up tomorrow."

Bruno hesitated, looking back at the office of the Wachtmeister. "Marius, are you sure that's a good idea?"

"What of it? Just because he's my old man doesn't mean a thing; he'll never be the wiser. So, do you want the ID or not?"

Bruno looked to Aleksy for confirmation; he slowly nodded and tried to appear a little worried for effect. After all, he didn't want to look too eager, or the German boys might get suspicious. "I'm in," he simply said.

Bruno escorted Aleksy to the photography shop where his image was captured without so much as one question from the photographer. After all, he'd found that "discretion" in this line of work was the best motto he could carry these days. Ultimately, "knowing nothing" had become the unspoken rule.

The next day, the boys returned to the photographer to pick up the photo. They left it with the young Marius as instructed, returning later that afternoon to retrieve what now had become Aleksy's official document. Upon opening the envelope, Aleksy did a double-take as his hands trembled with excitement. Yet, there it was in black and white; he was now Aleksander Rostek, "Hitler-Jugend" of the Third Reich. He quickly looked around as he slid the small card into his wallet, certain someone else was watching.

Chapter 5
Friends in Hidden Places

Aleksy quickly jumped into making plans with Bruno for their trip to the city, which would commence at 7 a.m. the next morning. Still, the young prisoner was busy turning the entire incident around in his mind, wondering how such a thing could have happened. How easy it had been to get a false ID. It was almost as if someone unknown to him was pulling strings. Some would say it was the "luck of the draw," others, a higher power. Although raised in a Catholic home, Aleksy didn't give much thought to supernatural intervention. He was simply satisfied with a "lucky card" that bore his name, Hitler-Jugend or not. And right now, the only thing he had to explain was his uncanny "luck" to the Polish sergeant looking out for him.

"What?" he bellowed out in anger. "How could you do this?"

"I did nothing!" replied Aleksy.

"Did you or did you not join the Hitler-Jugend?"

"Of course not! I am Polish! I would never side with the enemy!"

"Then how did you get such a document?"

"The Wachtmeister's son, and my friend Bruno got it for me!"

Aleksy studied the sergeant as the Polish man's anger began to subside. Then, he carefully went on to relay answers to the man's questions.

"Who knows how you got this document?" the sergeant demanded.

"My friend Bruno and the police officer's son."

The sergeant momentarily weighed this information in his mind then seemed to take refuge in the fact that it had not been widely circulated. Somewhat satisfied, he instructed Aleksy to hide the ID and not let anyone know about it. So, Aleksy did just that. He buried it beneath a loose board in his room.

The next day, early on a Sunday morning, Aleksy and his friend Bruno, escorted Bruno's mother onto the train without incident and to the city hospital to visit her convalescing brother.

Upon their arrival to the city, Aleksy was instructed to go to the nearby park and wait for his friend who would meet him there, and then together the boys would tour the city. Aleksy was quite impressed how his fake ID seemed to open doors for him. He would have to get the details straight on Bruno's uncle so that Herr Fat Farmer would think he had indeed visited the man. But, for now, he sat down on a grassy embankment to wait. From a comfortable position, he passed the time people-watching.

There were children, young people and old, couples and loners, stepping quickly through the park or strolling slowly, taking time to enjoy a bit of nature. Aleksy's attention was abruptly drawn to two young men as they made their way past him. Their conversation drifted on the gentle breeze toward the watching boy. Suddenly, Aleksy jumped up realizing he was hearing his native tongue.

"Excuse me," he called out. "Who are you?"

A look of surprise shifted between the two men bewildered as they heard their own Polish language being spoken to them.

"Are you a Pole?" they asked.

"Yes," replied the boy.

"How come you don't wear the letter 'P' on your jacket?"

Aleksy's eyes fell on the large "P" on the left side of their outerwear.

"How'd you get here?" came the questions in rapid fire. "Which labor camp are you in? How long have you been here? How come you don't wear the Polish label..."

Aleksy briefly explained how he was a "foster child" brought from Warsaw by the Germans to a nearby village. The two Polish men nodded, then explained how they were taken by the Gestapo from a Polish church and brought there to work. They lived in a factory camp outside the city limits, and if they worked hard and behaved, they were given a four hour pass to actually come into the city on Sundays.

The two eventually excused themselves, and Aleksy watched as they conversed with one another in the shade of an old Norway

Maple, occasionally looking his way. Soon they returned explaining that there was a Polish gentleman in civilian clothes who meets with them from time to time. They clarified that, during their meetings, he would make a point to ask them about their work in the factory and how they were treated by the Germans. Although they insisted to Aleksy that they knew nothing about this man, they felt he would be interested in talking with their new acquaintance. The man's surname was Pruski, and the two prisoners rightly suspected that he was a Polish officer. After securing Aleksy's address, the prisoners went on their way just as Bruno returned looking for his friend.

Although the sights and sounds of the German city would have been of interest to any young person, it was the incident in the park that held Aleksy's attention. As he and his side-kick wandered the streets looking at store fronts, watching civilians and military personnel, including SS men in black, Aleksy's mind occasionally wandered back to the two men. Was it possible that they held the key to his imminent escape? Did they know more than they had been willing to share? Would he ever hear from them again? And most of all, could they be trusted?

The summer passed and soon turned into fall without any answers. A full year had now gone by since Aleksy had seen his home village. Meanwhile, on the advice of his Polish sergeant and comrade, Aleksy continued living a quiet life as a prisoner of the Third Reich never knowing when liberation or escape might come. He busied himself supplying the prisoners with the coveted German newspapers and tending to the farmer's horses. Little by little, his patience finally paid off in late September, not long after Lars had reported for duty somewhere near Berlin.

As Aleksy led the horses along a now almost empty beach, a stranger approached him. He introduced himself as Mr. Pruski and stated that he'd learned about the boy from two Polish men serving as forced laborers in the city. He explained that he and another officer were working together in that same location and were wondering if Aleksy would be interested in leaving the farm to work for a man who ran a food distributing company in the city. He was looking for several young boys to work in his business.

"Yes, I *would* be interested," replied Aleksy, "but what about my German guardian?"

"He's the least of your worries," said Pruski. "There are more important things to be concerned about."

"Still, I would like to talk with my Polish friend who is also held prisoner here. He's a sergeant in the military, and he's been a tremendous help to me."

"I"m sorry, but it's important not to involve others." he replied. "You wouldn't want your friend to be forced to rat you out, would you?"

"Of course not."

"So, how did you ever come by a Hitler Youth ID?"

"How do you know about that?"

Mr. Pruski smiled. "We have our ways; we just don't disclose them."

So, Aleksy slowly described how his friend, Bruno, had helped him get the ID although the Polish sergeant had not approved. He explained that under the sergeant's direction he had hidden it away where no one would see it. Shrugging his shoulders, he admitted that his German friend who had provided the false identification obviously had not been near as concerned as the Polish sergeant.

Pruski smiled. "Your friends did a huge favor for you without even knowing it," he said. "Does anyone else know about this?"

"No one," the boy confirmed with confidence. "No one except for Bruno, the Wachtmeister's son, and of course, the sergeant."

"Have the Hitler-Jugend contacted you?"

"No, sir."

"Good. Do you have access to a Hitler-Jugend uniform?"

Aleksy blinked. "Why would I need that?"

"To go with your ID card, of course."

The Polish boy thought a moment. He knew that Lars had left a month ago to return to military duty. Is It possible that he would have left a uniform here for safe keeping? Perhaps a dress uniform? One for propaganda parades?

"I know where I can look," he finally said, "but there are no guarantees."

"OK," replied Pruski. "Start there. If you find one, put it in your satchel and carry it with you. That way you'll appear to be on leave if anyone questions your documentation as a Hitler Youth. Otherwise, I will get one for you after you arrive in the city."

"Yes sir," responded Aleksy, his mind already scheming.

"Do the things you normally do, but don't tell anybody including your sergeant that you have talked with me nor that you plan to escape."

Aleksy gave the man his word then bid him farewell, watching the mysterious stranger trudge away through the sand. He shook his head trying to clear it, but more specifically trying to make sense of just *how* he could be so lucky. Perhaps the Virgin Mary was smiling on him as a result of the few masses his parents had dragged him to. And what a smart boy he had been for taking the horses to the beach that very day. He grinned, radiating with self-pride.

For the next seven months, Aleksy did as Mr. Pruski had instructed. He continued to work in the barn and washed the horses on a regular basis obediently serving in whatever way was expected while secretly and patiently awaiting Pruski's return.

As he waited, he closely watched for the farmer's wife to leave the house, so he could visit the room in which Lars slept, something he'd have to figure out once he gained access into the building. His opportunity finally came when both the farmer and his wife attended the wedding of a niece in another village. Although spring weddings were the norm, the bride's prospective husband happened to be home on leave, and it was decided the nuptials should be held immdiately not knowing when he might get another pass. And as luck would have it, the farmer instructed Aleksy to keep the parlor stove hot while they were away.

The boy promptly reported at noon as ordered. Upon entering the house, which for the most part had remained foreign to the uninvited guest, he cautiously passed through the kitchen noticing the pink apron Romana had worn before giving it to Aleksy who had danced a jig on that ill-fated day. Aleksy often struggled with the fact that that was one time he had not been so lucky, unless he considered the fact that he had not been shot on the spot which was often the norm with the SS.

He pushed the door open to the parlor and spotted the potbellied stove centered in the middle of the room with its heat radiating to every corner. After checking the coals, he stood up and slowly perused the room. Two doors indicated two other rooms, one of which he assumed would be used by Lars. He cautiously opened the first one and took in the bed, chest of drawers and cosmetics on a bureau. Satisfied this was not the right room, he quietly closed the door then opened the other. It too held the essentials, but nothing of a feminine nature. For some reason, he paused and looked behind him before entering. He smirked at himself. "Stop acting like a coward," he whispered.

Aleksy stepped inside the room leaving the door ajar. A huge pine wardrobe beckoned to him from next to a lace curtained window; he hurried across the room and threw the closet door open. There were a few casual shirts and two pairs of everyday pants; and there, hanging against the inside wall, was the coveted Nazi uniform, complete with black pants and the famous brown shirt! The Polish boy couldn't believe his good luck. It just seemed to be unending. He reached out and pulled the uniform toward him, running his fingers over the regional patch and the swastika badge circling the left sleeve. And as he did so, he could sense a feeling of evil that made him shiver. Now, he had to figure out how to remove it from the house with no one noticing… He scanned the room searching for anything he might use to conceal his contraband.

The sound of an approaching truck alerted Aleksy that he might have to return later, but he'd come too far not to claim his prize. Noticing an empty box in one corner of the room, he grabbed it and began stuffing the uniform into what proved to be a small space. Suddenly, the sound of the truck came to a halt. He tore the uniform from the box and then quickly returned it to its original place, not sure what to do at this point. German voices conversed as two men emerged from the vehicle, both in Nazi uniforms. Aleksy tossed the too-small box back into the corner and peeped through the curtained window. He froze. Lars was home.

Chapter 6
Something about a Uniform

The community dance had been such fun! And what a great way to lift the spirits not only of the locally stationed military but of the local citizens as well. The war had gotten to everyone and most people were feeling somewhat relieved to have an opportunity to escape the seriousness of it, at least for a little while.

Elise waved at her aunt and uncle across the room who were caught up in the fast-paced swing music supplied by a popular band. Although a few years older than her own parents, they sure did have a lot of energy in spite of her uncle's diabetes. It had kept him out of the war, a fact that greatly grieved him. He was a patriot at heart and often felt embarrassed by his inability to serve. So, he made up for it by volunteering all he could on the home-front while maintaining a job in a textile factory. Meanwhile, it felt good seeing him have fun with Aunt Emma.

Her friend Ruth twirled in her direction, her skirt a colorful umbrella as she danced toward Elise carrying two cups of punch. Elise graciously accepted the offering while laughing at her silly friend who had sloshed punch onto the floor.

"Aren't you glad our parents allowed us to be junior hostesses for the USO?" asked the rosey cheeked Ruth.

"You bet! But from the looks of all these handsome men in uniform, I'd say they weren't going to allow it unless they could be here with us."

Ruth laughed and nodded toward the right where her own parents were kicking up *their* heels. She rolled her eyes. "Kind of embarrassing, but at least they're having a good time."

"Yep, and I guess they better while they can. Aunt Emma starts a job on Monday."

"You're kidding! Your aunt has always been a homemaker."

"And she's always wanted children, but things don't always go the way we think they should. Just look at me. I never dreamed I'd be coming to America all alone as a thirteen-year-old."

"Isn't there a Bible verse about that? Oh, yeah – something about how a man makes his plans but God directs his steps? But then again, the oldsters say dancing is a sin; I just don't get that one when David himself was a dancer."

Elise shrugged. "Maybe in war time it's ok?"

These Americans seemed to know a lot more about the Bible than Elise ever did. After all, wasn't that the job of a priest? He could just tell them what's there and save them a lot of work.

"Anyway," she continued, "Aunt Emma is going to be a 'Rosie the Riveter' at the ammo plant."

"Oh, wow!" exclaimed Ruth. "Wouldn't I love to do that! I bet I could rivet airplane wings single handedly!

"No doubt about it, Rufus," responded Elise, affectionately using her friend's nickname. "There's nothing you can't fix or do! But you know you have to finish school first, then you can think about being a Rosie the Riveter."

"I know, but I'd rather be doing things that matter for the war effort."

"Well, being a junior hostess at the USO is an important job. Just look at how you help raise the morale of these guys heading to and from war. Sometimes they just need someone to talk to, and you're the best listener of anyone I know. And how about your Victory Garden?"

Ruth beamed. "Well, it is coming along rather nicely. Actually, we have a bumper crop of green beans! Need any?"

"Uh, no thanks," replied Elise turning up her lip. "I've eaten enough French beans to last me a lifetime."

Ruth laughed. "Well, these are good 'ol American string beans!"

"No thanks. You can keep your beans *and* strings. But I have noticed that you don't have one single weed in your garden and look at all the produce you've canned to help your family. I'm afraid my little patch of a Victory Garden looks like it surrendered to the enemy a long time ago!"

With that, both girls laughed and turned back to watching the older folks dancing the night away.

Elise wished her own parents could be there dancing and forgetting about this terrible war. She hadn't heard from her mom for a while which was worrisome, but she prayed for them faithfully, for their safety and that this terrible war would come to an end soon.

Ruth nudged her with her elbow, "Isn't that Mid over there dancing with that sailor boy?"

"Yep, and there's Merle right behind her twin with a soldier boy."

"I think all those girls do is dance! They must have been born kicking their chubby little feet."

Elise turned toward someone lightly tapping on her shoulder. It was a sailor she'd noticed earlier blatantly smiling at her. Elise returned his smile.

"Hey, pretty girl, would you like to dance?"

"Why, it would be a privilege to dance with someone defending the world against Hitler!" Handing her punch cup to Ruth she winked, then headed toward the dance floor.

~~~~~~~

The next day, Ruth wasn't surprised at all when Elise stopped by to tell her that the sailor boy had asked her out on a date.

"So, your aunt and uncle are actually allowing you to go?" she asked.

"Well, they met Willie last night, and after drilling him with a thousand questions, they felt he'd be safe enough. Anyway, we're just going for ice cream. It's not like some kind of huge date or anything."

"But still…."

"Enough about me! Did that handsome soldier you were eyeing ever dance with you?"
~~~~~~~

"He did! Just a couple of times, but it was fun, and he was really nice. He's from Virginia and on his way to Europe; his boat launches day after tomorrow."

"Any chance you might write to him or see him when he gets back?"

"Afraid not. He has a girlfriend back home and wedding plans are in the making. He was just looking for some friendly conversation."

"Wouldn't you know? All the cute ones are already taken."

"Yep," confirmed Ruth. "Hey, when's your date for ice cream?"

"Tonight at The Creamery, but I won't need a chaperone!"

"Hint well taken, my friend. Have fun!"

Elise laughed and bid her friend farewell then walked toward the high rise apartment she shared with her aunt and uncle. Lifting her gaze to the bright blue sky, she peeped between the city's tall buildings. Same sky her parents could see. For some reason, it was the sky that brought comfort and helped her endure. One day she'd take to that sky in an airplane and see her parents again. How she missed them, especially Maman. Still, Aunt Emma had done her best to develop a warm relationship with her "foster" daughter, and Elise loved her for it. It's just that a daughter, no matter how old, always needed her mama.

She sighed turning her thoughts back to her upcoming date with Willie. She didn't really know what it was, but there was just something about a military uniform. It could, no doubt, make a person do some pretty crazy things. Elise picked up her step.

Chapter 7
A Time to Run

Once he had returned the uniform to its original place, Aleksy knew he had to stay calm. His mind began to click as the voices got closer to the door. He could hurry to the parlor and be caught stirring the fire as instructed, or he could crawl beneath the bed and hide out until Lars left. Neither scenario seemed too promising, but he could better explain himself being next to the stove than found under the bed.

Lars and his friend entered the kitchen as Aleksy stepped into the parlor and quietly pulled the stove door open. When they entered the parlor, he was using the poker to stoke the fire. Lars simply nodded toward him then in German told his friend, "This is the Polish slave I was telling you about."

The other man laughed. "Your brother-in-law was smart to bring a peasant home from Warsaw. But he doesn't look very strong. You should feed him more."

Aleksy continued stoking the fire, pretending he couldn't understand a word.

"So, where is the little German maid that used to be here?" the unknown Nazi continued. " I wouldn't mind having a little sport with her."

Lars rolled his eyes. "Really, Aldo. Sometimes I wonder why I even bother with you. She was nothing but a peasant and was dismissed as soon as she was found entertaining the Polish boy. Actually, she was in the process of helping him escape."

"Really!" exclaimed Aldo.

"Yes, the Polish slave was caught red handed with the key to his quarters; she had evidently just handed it to him when I came into the room."

Aldo laughed. "They wouldn't make for good German spies, huh?"

"Stay here," responded Lars, "I'll get that other uniform I need."

Lars disappeared into his bedroom while Aldo walked around the parlor picking up framed photographs and studying them. Aleksy continued to stoke the fire and added a little more coal from the metal box sitting next to the stove. Just as he was about to exit the room, Lars returned.

"Stoppen!" he commanded Aleksy. Aleksy turned and looked at the German wondering what was to come next. The German mimicked drinking and eating. He obviously wanted the Pole to prepare food and drink for his guest. Aleksy sighed as he pushed the parlor door open that led to the kitchen. He knew better than to disregard orders from an SS agent, especially this one. So, he went about gathering potatoes, cabbage and sausages which he proceeded to fry in one large pan. As for their thirst, water would have to do.

Lars and his friend came into the kitchen laughing over a private joke. The fat farmer's brother-in-law walked immediately to the cook stove and leaned his head over the frying pan sniffing in an exaggerated fashion.

"Perhaps the Pole can cook," he laughed, addressing Aldo. "But you're not in uniform," he continued, looking at Aleksy this time. With a flourish, he approached the pink apron and pulled it from its hook. Turning to Aleksy, he grinned in such a way that the Polish boy wanted nothing more than to slug him. But he knew he couldn't as such a move would greatly hinder his plans for escape.

The Germans laughed hysterically as Lars pulled the girly apron over Aleksy's head. Aleksy could feel his face turning pink to match the fabric as both anger and embarrassment spread up his neck into his cheeks. Or perhaps it was hatred.

The two men positioned themselves at the little kitchen table where Aleksy and Romana had shared many a meal. Jovially, they clapped their hands and called to the boy to serve them.

"Kleiner Bär!" Lar's friend called out, using the German endearment for Little Bear. "Please bring food to me. I am so tired from fighting in the war, and I need to see a pretty face."

Lars hooted at this then snapped his fingers. "Hurry, Schätzchen! I might die waiting for you."

Aleksy slammed plates in front of the two men. "I am not your sweetie," he retorted in Polish to Lars, "and the sooner you die, the better."

The Germans doubled over in laughter finding his anger to their liking although they had no clue what he'd just said. Aleksy jerked the offensive apron over his head and threw it on the floor before storming out of the house. The echo of their dimming laughter was accentuated with the slam of the door. Aleksy stomped toward the barn to cool down.

He shrugged at how short-lived his good luck had been, but then reminded himself that at least he *hadn't* gotten caught holding the Nazi uniform. "So, I am indeed very lucky," he stated to himself. He grinned, aware that his quick thinking to shove the uniform back into the wardrobe and step into the parlor was what had saved his neck. Yes, Alesky Rostek was indeed self-sufficient. He believed he'd make it out of Germany alive whenever the precise time came.

Fall and winter came and went with no word from Mr. Pruski. Meanwhile, the bitter cold and lack of coal during the winter season was especially difficult for the Polish prisoners who shivered endlessly in their less than adequate dwelling. Yet, the young Aleksy warmed himself with the thought that the mysterious Mr. Pruski would one day return, and with his return would come the ticket to his freedom. In what form that ticket would come, Aleksy wasn't sure, but anything beat remaining a prisoner to the Germans. He was Polish, not German, and he intended to return to his home and heritage when the conditions were right.

Aleksy continued to play the role of a good prisoner as the wheels of his freedom were being set in motion. Along with the other prisoners, he now delivered coal from the farmer's property, which boasted its own natural resource. Against the bitter winter winds, he and his comrades lugged the heavy sacks to the homes they supplied, adding even more coins to the farmer's pockets. Yet once again, Aleksy's patience paid off when one April day Mr. Pruski reappeared on the beach.

The man nonchalantly made his way toward the lad who was busy washing his overseer's horses. As he approached, the boy continued to work.

" It's finally time for you to run away," Pruski stated in a low voice. "Listen closely to the instructions I'm about to give you."

Aleksy listened intently, keeping his eyes on the sudsy horse.

"You must be ready to leave by the first of next month," said Pruski. "You will take the early train to the city as you did when you journeyed there with your friend. Upon your arrival, you will spend the morning in the same park where you met the Polish factory workers. That afternoon, you will go to the Salvation Army, located two streets south of the park, where you will stay overnight."

Aleksy nodded as he continued to scrub, visualizing the city in his head.

"Your story will be that while visiting your ailing grandmother, you missed your train. The workers at the Salvation Army will put you up for the night and see that you're fed. Memorize the address there because you will need to know it when you go to the employment office the next day; it will serve as your home address."

"When you arrive at the employment office, go to the third window only. Tell the lady that you'd like to work for a company that specializes in wholesale foods, and give her your actual name as there are already a lot of Polish names in Prussia. When she has finished asking questions, you are to sit and wait for the business owner to come interview you."

~~~~~~~

As the calendar marched toward the first of the month, Aleksy prepared for his soon departure from the residence of Herr Fat Farmer. It had been his home now for the past two and a half years. With great excitement he anticipated the day he would hop the train to freedom. But meanwhile, he had some patriotic business to which he needed to attend.
~~~~~~~

Aleksy knew full well part of his new life would involve the underground transport of arms to Poland and her allies. Such knowledge excited him all the more. He even took what little money he had and purchased a Colt 1911 through contacts provided by Pruski himself. He knew it was a major risk in such a small village, but he was determined that if he were to live out his days on the enemy's turf, he'd at least live them out serving the home team. He even snuck off to a secluded part of the beach to try out the illegal weapon he'd so successfully attained. Meanwhile, Mr. Pruski was delighted in the confirmation that Aleksy's unique bravery and personality would serve as strong assets to the underground work of the allies.

Aleksy mentally checked over the list of verbal instructions he'd received from Pruski. It was something he'd done numerous times since his meeting on the beach, but he wanted to make sure everything was just right. This could prove to be his only opportunity for escape, and he didn't intend to muddle it up like he did with Romana and the "key" incident. He refused to spend the rest of his life sudsing foul smelling work horses. The boy wiped his sweaty palms on his pant leg smiling victoriously. He was ready for adventure even if the thought made him perspire.

Ultimately, getting away from the farm to the train proved to be easy enough. He'd simply taken off, never entertaining the thought that he wouldn't make it to the train or for that matter, to freedom. No one had seemed to notice him leaving the farm except one of the dogs he'd befriended which trotted beside him a few feet, happily wagging his tail. Aleksy patted him on the head, "Keep your fat master content," he said, "so you won't end up in his frying pan." He laughed at his own joke then looking over his shoulder one last time to make sure no one was watching, he hitched up his trousers and headed in the direction of the train station.

Once at the train station, the boy had simply shown his ID as a Hitler Juegend to the station master who flipped through several files. "Ah, here you go," he finally said, smiling and handing him a ticket that had been reserved by Mr. Pruski. "So, returning to base after leave?"

Aleksy nodded and smiled.

"Where are you stationed, son?"

"Berlin," Aleksy replied, hoping there would be no more questions.

The kind man nodded. "Thank you for your service to the Third Reich," he said saluting Aleksy.

"Yes, sir." Aleksy saluted in return as he knew it'd be expected then turned away to board the train.

Aleksy's easy departure was made possible by the stroke of good luck he'd come to expect. If he were to miss anything about his two and a half years confined on a German farm, it would be the dogs for their kind companionship in his early weeks spent there. And of course, his Polish sergeant who would be proud to know Aleksy's moment had come. He wished he could have said goodbye; he owed a lot to his mentor. He leaned back into his seat and dozed off until the screeching brakes of the iron caravan interrupted his sleep.

Stepping off the train, Aleksy's eyes scanned his surroundings which now felt a bit familiar due to his earlier visit there. He headed toward the park where he would spend the morning napping and people watching, pretending to be free and allowing himself to enjoy the luxury of the feeling, believing that today was just the beginning of the liberation to come. Looking up, Aleksy judged the time by the sun as it rose higher into the eastern sky, finally arcing downward toward the western landscape, giving the signal to seek out his next location.

He then made his way to the Salvation Army with little help, and upon his arrival, Aleksy found a warm welcome by those eager to assist. His story of visiting an ailing grandmother was received with compassion and kindness. Of course, he could stay there, as anyone who served the elderly community in wartime was considered a friend of the Salvation Army! The boy filled his stomach from a bountiful supply of food then bedded down in his assigned quarters, no longer to dream as he'd done on the train, but to rest and refuel his strength for whatever lay ahead.

He arrived at the "Arbeitsamt", or employment office, shortly after nine o'clock the next day, just as Pruski had instructed. Quickly locating the third window, he approached it with confidence, introducing himself as Aleksander Rostek and explaining how he was looking for a company where he could learn the wholesale food business. The lady behind the window instructed Aleksy to have a seat. So, he did, unsure of what was to come next. It was here that he waited and waited and waited…

Finally, an older gentleman entered the room and approached the third window. He chatted with the woman then turned from his conversation long enough to look at the boy. After collecting a stack of papers, he made his way toward Aleksy and introduced himself as Herr Lezon, the owner of a wholesale business which sold foods to local stores throughout the city.

He handed the teenager a booklet, the *Arbeitsbuch,* issued by the third Reich, which served as an ID and work permit. Its contents would hold a log of Aleksy's work history as a German citizen. "Always keep this book in a safe place where you can get to it," said the aged man. "And when you travel anywhere, make sure it's with you."

Aleksy immediately studied the small booklet, flipping through its thirty-plus pages. Turning it over in his hands, he could feel the promise of freedom pulsing through his palms.

"You will be part of several boys working here," the man continued as he explained that the position was that of an apprenticeship. He then beckoned Aleksy to follow him to an undisclosed location. The boy looked around taking in his surroundings; one could never be too sure.

They entered a private office where Herr Lezon introduced his protege to a lady responsible for overseeing the building. After consulting a chart, she assigned Aleksy to a room that would now be home to him.

"I will talk more with you later," said the older man. "I have it on good authority that you will work well in this business. However, the important thing is not to ask too many questions as this can get you or others in trouble; just act as any other citizen of the Third Reich, and tell the other boys as little as possible about yourself."

Aleksy nodded his head mesmerized over what he had gotten himself into. He was about to enjoy the exploits of a teenage spy! If only Koby could be with him to share in this adventure. But then he recalled the memory of his sobbing friend as he'd been dragged away by the Gestapo. He shook his head briskly, better not go there. Yet, it had been over two years since he'd last seen his best friend, and he couldn't help but wonder how he was doing.

The next morning, Aleksy was taken to an order processing center where he was instructed on how to package orders for small retail stores. He simply put the requested items into boxes and labeled them. As he stealthily worked, Herr Lezon checked on him several times and seemed pleased with his progress. The other boys working beside him were more intent on their own work than on who Aleksy was. Not once did they ask where he was from. He shrugged it off with a bit of relief, possibly they, too, were hiding their own identities.

As the days progressed, Mr. Pruski often appeared and reassured Aleksy that his work was on target. Aleksy was glad to hear this as it was starting to get a little mundane; he was more than ready for some excitement. Much to the boy's relief, Mr. Pruski finally asked his new employee to meet him that evening for supper. Aleksy was curious to hear what the unpredictable man might tell him, but at the same time, he felt an element of restlessness.

The young scout could sense the blood of patriotism blubbing through his veins. He could feel it stirring in his very soul, confirming his love for his country and fellow man. He believed with great depth that this was the same feeling many a Polish man encountered when he took a position in the underground military. It was no doubt the same feeling that was set into motion long before Warsaw's surrender. Going underground required "taking an oath of obedience and secrecy" and then backing that oath with one's very life. The young Aleksy was more than ready as he approached the appointed eatery in anticipation.

Once the two men were settled in a nearby restaurant, Pruski leaned forward and spoke in a low voice across the table.

"I need to send you on a mission to help transport pistols to our underground soldiers in Warsaw."

The younger man nodded, waiting for Pruski to continue.

"You will need to wear a Hitler-Jugend uniform which I will provide unless you already have one."

Aleksy shook his head. "No sir," he said, "but I tried."

"Not a problem," responded Pruski. "I'll see that one is sent to you right away. Once you have received it, put it on and take the first train to Polessk. Do not even think about sitting with the civilians; they ask too many questions of the Hitler-Jugend and you might trip up. The pistols will be placed in a locker on the east wall at the Polessk train station. Use this key to open it," he said handing over a small metal key with the numbers 432 engraved on it. "You'll find a military knapsack inside the locker, but don't open the knapsack. The pistols will be inside of it; you'll know from the weight. Replace it with an empty knapsack you'll be given.

"If you're asked where you're going, say that you're going to Warsaw to serve as a guard at the former capital building for the Fuhrer. Paperwork will be provided just in case they want to check your credentials. After swapping out the knapsacks, return to the ticket window and purchase a ticket for your return trip here. Any questions?"

Aleksy studied the older man, digesting the information he'd just been given. He knew it was an easy assignment and he'd have no problems. However, the biggest challenge would be staying clear of the Gestapo. Final arrangements were made and a meal consumed before the two men bid one another farewell. Young Aleksander Rostek, was now officially a member of the underground Polish resistance. His German friends had indeed done him a favor by providing a Hitler-Jugend ID bearing his name. One never knew what identify he might need from day to day. Aleksy wondered if he would even know just *who* he was by the time the war ended, if it ever did.

Aleksy looked around the restaurant before exiting. Had some unknown person witnessed their meeting? Maybe they'd seen the delivery of a small key? If not, why did it feel as if someone were watching? He hurried out the door into the darkness.

Chapter 8
Caught!

Aleksy's first assignment with the underground proved to be a success, leading to even more missions for the resistance movement. And needless to say, the teenager was feeling pretty good about himself. In addition to getting the guns to Warsaw, he diligently tracked supply trains to Russia, reporting to Mr. Pruski the time of the transports leaving East Prussia. Aleksy's job of transporting weaponry quickly transferred into one of collecting intelligence and pinpointing German military facilities for sabotage. All went well … until his arrest in December.

The irony of it all was that Aleksy was on the very same mission he'd been sent on his first time out - to the train station in Polessk. As was his habit, he boarded the city train then sat away from the civilians as instructed and busied himself with reading or watching the scenery slide past. He was in the process of pouring over *Mein Kampf* when he felt someone sit next to him. Aleksy looked up, to find a member of the Gestapo smiling at him.

"Ah, I see you are interested in our great Fuhrer," he said nodding at the book in Aleksy's hand.

Aleksy forced himself to smile at the intruding figure. "One cannot help being interested. He has an amazing mind."

"Yes, and to think that he is now carrying out the very ideas first published in a book he penned many years ago. The man definitely has fortitude."

"All Germans should be required to read it."

"I agree fully, especially when I saw the opposing book titles Germans were already reading. I must say, I was quite happy to see both religious and modern liberal books destroyed at a recent book burning. They had to be banned you know; Hitler's politics and philosophies are all that's needed for the greater good of Germany."

Aleksy nodded, hesitant to disagree.

"So, soldier, where are you headed?"

"I've received orders to go to Warsaw, to the capital building."

"Good for you, young man, You know that is considered an honor – to serve at the government buildings."

"Yes, it is indeed. I was quite surprised to find I'd been chosen to do so."

"Well, Hitler wants only his best in such places. As for me, my orders are always among the Jewish areas in the cities and more recently, the ghettos. I'm not complaining, mind you, but it can get pretty depressing purging those places night after night. I guess the best part is the power I feel when I storm into someone's house who thinks I have no idea as to what they've been up to. That's when I feel like I'm really helping Hitler by cleaning up Germany and returning her to the way she used to be before so many 'undesirables' ruined this great nation."

Aleksy grew weary of the man's conversation as he went on and on, but had to feign otherwise. By the time the train stopped in Polessk, he thought he'd go crazy pretending to support the ideas of an overbearing Nazi. Aleksy finally stood and reached for his bag after wishing the man a good day. From his peripheral vision, he watched him move down the aisle and off the train. It was a huge relief to see him go.

The boy headed to the rows of lockers and dug out his key bearing number 432. He placed it in the key hole and turned it to the left. Then sticking his hand in, he pulled out the knapsack bearing the contraband pistols and replaced it with the empty one, shut the door and turned the key to the right ready for the return trip. As he rotated on his heel to leave, he smacked into the uniformed man who had shared his seat on the train.

The man put his hands on Aleksy's shoulders either to steady him or keep him from running off. He grinned into the boy's face as he reached for the knapsack. "Did you really think I didn't know what you were up to? I've had my eye on you, boy, and I knew it was just a matter of time. You have a friend who's looking for you."

Aleksy soon learned that Herr Fat Farmer was not happy that he'd slipped away from the farm and had spent many weeks looking for him. The man had immediately filed a report for his arrest; he wanted his slave labor back. However, his offense was not only that of escaping from the farm, but for being in possession of a gun while in the village. Aleksy admitted that possession of the weapon was true, but it had only been purchased to send to those in the resistance, a fact he couldn't hardly relay to the Gestapo.

The young escapee was quickly deposited into a prison within the city to await his trial. Herr Lezon visited him there.

"What have you done to call this attention to yourself, Aleksy?" he asked in a low voice.

"I was serving the underground by delivering a weapon, a Colt 1911 if you must know."

"So, who knew about this besides you?"

"Mr. Pruski and the contacts he gave me."

"But his contacts are thoroughly checked, so I can't imagine a German getting hold of this. Do they know this handgun was purchased for the Polish Home Army?"

"I don't think so; they just knew I had possession of it."

"But where did it actually come from?"

"The black market. Where does anything come from these days?"

"Ssh! Keep your voice down! There are ears everywhere," hissed Lezon. "Do you even know *who* you were dealing with?"

"Of course not! The gun and the money I paid were exchanged on a back road near the farm. I left the money in an empty culvert, and the gun was there the next day."

"So, what did you do with it after you picked it up?"

"I wanted to see how well it shot, so I fired it on a secluded part of the beach."

Herr Lezon stared at the boy as if in shock. "I hope you're jesting," he said.

"No, sir. I'm not."

"To be so intelligent, that was not only dumb but risky as well!"

Aleksy hung his head.

"My plan is to get you out of here as soon as possible, but what you have just told me may result in further arrests even after you leave here."

Aleksy nodded.

"Meanwhile, don't waste your brain on worrisome thoughts. You can't undo the past or foolish decisions. I'll get you out of here, but it'll take a little while." With that, he stood up and called for the guard.

Aleksy used his imprisonment to reflect, to plan, connive and play out various scenarios, the possible "what ifs". While Aleksy's mind worked at how to win the battle against his opponents, the strategic game he played was not a game at all. It was real life, and the winner was the one who lived. Without a doubt, Aleksy knew that he alone would be that winner. There was no other option.

Herr Lezon finally came through on his promise, and the boy was released two months later. His trial had been delayed, and the only explanation he could muster up for his release was that Herr Lezon's connection through his family business must have provided ample supply of the much coveted chocolates and coffees to the Reich's German officers. They may have been the only bargaining power this dissident needed.

Immediately upon his release, Aleksy was ordered to travel to England and join up with the Polish Air Force. This was to Aleksy's liking and two weeks later, the approval for his departure to England came through. The now *Major* Pruski wished the boy good luck, and Herr Lezon gave him a supply of food ration cards along with enough money to get to southern France. There, he would board an allied ship heading to England. But first, Aleksy would travel eighteen days through Nazi Germany.

Dressed in his Hitler Youth uniform, Aleksy could easily pull off the role of any German boy. And on this long trip, he had plenty of time to practice. His first stop was his childhood village in Poland. It had been a little over two and a half years since he'd last seen his home or his family. He was definitely ready for a taste of the familiar. However, when he arrived, the familiar was not to be found. A German family now occupied what *used* to be called "home." Although disappointed, he didn't even attempt to gain entrance.

In his walk through once familiar streets, the teenager came across one member of his former Boy Scout troop who had not left the city with the others when the Germans arrived. Aleksy could see the boy was shocked by his Hitler-Jugend uniform.

"Aleksy?" It was a question accentuated with large eyes.

"Hello, Stefan," came the reply. "How have you been?"

"Um, fine…considering."

"Things aren't the same here."

"No, not since the N-Nazis came," he stuttered, leery of his friend's attire.

"Yeah, I guess it's all been a matter of survival." Aleksy replied, hoping he hadn't hinted too much with his double meaning.

Stefan swallowed a lump in his throat. "But not *everyone* survived. My Tatus died in the battle at Warsaw."

Aleksy dropped his eyes to the ground suddenly feeling strange in his Nazi garb. "I'm sorry Stefan. Your father was a good man."

"And I guess you heard about Koby?"

Aleksy quickly raised his head again. "No, what of him?"

"They sent him to Lebensborn to make him one of them." Aleksy's friend paused obviously disturbed by having to relay this information to a young man in a German uniform. "Only he had too much Polish blood in him and refused to accept their warped beliefs. So they beat him . . . until he died."

Aleksy could feel water forming around the rims of his eyes. Koby, his boyhood friend, dreamer of Juro Janosik capers and the fastest bike racer in all the village. Aleksy pictured his friend on the Warsaw soccer field, crying shamelessly as he said his goodbyes. Yet, he had died a patriot refusing to become one of *them*. He had died strong.

Suddenly Aleksy wanted to run away, scream and cry, at least rip off the disgusting uniform he wore in order to save himself. He wished the train had never stopped here. He nodded at his friend who now had tears streaming down his own face, and then turned and walked away lest he, too, give in to the emotions he'd managed to beat down. His country needed him, not his tears.

From his home village, he traveled to Berlin where he spent two days in a Hitler Youth hostel. In a time when secrecy meant survival, Aleksy was relieved that no unnecessary questions were asked by the Nazi boys who bunked with him. An explanation that he was traveling to Austria to visit an uncle and his counterfeit badges of higher rank, no doubt, contributed to curbing any further conversation. He continued on to Munich, and from there, to Austria, where he could practically feel the cool breeze of Switzerland. Yet as he moved, his plans took a sharp turn.

Attempting to cross the German border from Austria into Switzerland, Aleksy found himself face to face with German guards. They promptly made arrangements to transfer him to the local Gestapo headquarters for deposition.

"Sir," he explained to the Gestapo officer, "I have not had opportunity to travel much and was quite taken by the medieval scenery in the village. Because of the distraction, I ended up going the wrong way. My plan is to head toward Berlin where I'm stationed."

The officer looked skeptical. "A German boy of the Third Reich can lose his way in his homeland? I think you're lying. Your features alone belie you. I believe you are Polish."

"No sir. I'm telling you the truth. I'm a simple country boy who has had little opportunity to travel. But now, thanks to our great Fuhrer, I am able to see the world."

"You are a disgrace to our great Fuhrer!"

Raising his club above his own head, the man slammed it into Aleksy's skull then preceded to beat him with a vengeance out of the portals of Hell. He continued his hatred and aggression toward the young imposter by ripping off the Hitler-Jugend uniform leaving it in shreds.

"How dare you, a Pole, dress in the Hitler Youth uniform!" he shrieked.

The unarmed teenager tucked his head into his arms in a small attempt to stave off the repetitive blows.

Following the beating and a transfer to the local prison which looked like an old fortress, Aleksy was left on his own. The building was located inside a courtyard that also held a police station, all encircled by a foreboding wall. It was in these surroundings that he simply sat and waited.

Two days later the officer received a return wire stating that Aleksy had already been in jail on charges of having owned a pistol in a village near the Baltic Sea. Had Herr Lezon's chocolates and coffees been available at that moment, Aleksy knew there would not have been enough to bribe the hard core commitment that pulsated through the veins of these particularly dedicated Nazis.

Although the traveled miles, now lost to his confinement in prison, would have devastated many a man of stout heart, it only served to strengthen the young Aleksander Rostek. For in his heart of hearts he knew that he, like the Nazis, would still stand proud for *his* own country, and that he would eventually see freedom. He would do it in the memory of his best friend, Koby.

Then and there, Aleksy determined he would depend on no one but himself to get him through. Yet, for all his "smarts", he was still oblivious to the fact he was allowed passage in one place and denied it in another. Polish pride and youthful arrogance seemed to serve as blinders to what was actually going on around him. For just as he had often sensed, the Nazis weren't the only ones with eyes on this Polish boy. There was much more to the story.

Chapter 9
In Need of a Miracle

Aleksy found himself sharing a cell with six other boys, mostly Austrian who did not want to join the Hitler Youth program or who were draft dodgers refusing to serve in the German army. He would spend several weeks with his new comrades while awaiting the arrival of a prisoner transport that would return him to his former jurisdiction. Meanwhile, the Germans would make good use of one more laborer in processing damaged Nazi apparel into new German uniforms.

Aleksy worked in the prison basement alongside his cell mates separating linings and metal buttons from torn and bloodied military attire. They used knives and pliers to cut off the buttons. The room in which they worked, located beneath the prison court, had only one window; the bottom half lay underground while the upper part of the window was above ground, allowing light to flow from a space created by the adjoining courtyard. A man standing guard at the large door of the courtyard entry could be viewed by the prisoners from the barred basement window.

While all the boys were kind to Aleksy, it was Danek, the oldest, the leader and supervisor of the group, with whom Aleksy became close friends. Knowing that Aleksy was to be transferred to another jurisdiction, the older boy advised him not to mention to the other boys why he was being held prisoner or even why he wanted to escape to Switzerland. It was best to keep information at a minimum as one could not be certain just which side some Austrians were on. Just like several of the prisoners, the prison guards were all Austrian except for the German who manned the office. Danek, an Austrian, expected to be drafted into the German army and was furious about it. As Aleksy was not any happier, the two friends planned and put into motion their escape.

"Guard, guard!" called out Danek.

"What do you want?" came the reply with the sound of heavy boots.

"One of the prisoners is sick and needs attention!"

"So, what do you think I am? A doctor?"

Aleksy waited in the shadows, clutching tightly to a confiscated knife from the basement work area.

"I was hoping you could send for help," continued Danek. "The boy is very sick and could possibly die."

"Then just one less dirty Austrian to feed," came the curt response.

"Sir, do you have no feeling for humankind?"

"For humankind, yes. Austrian dogs, no. You are traitors."

"Because we refuse to be forced to serve in another man's military does not make us traitors."

"Ah, but your great leader is of Austrian blood, and you've turned your back on him."

Danek tilted his face and spit on the filthy floor. "Adolf is no leader of mine."

"But that's where you are wrong. Your people were once part of the German confederation, although they won't admit it. The Fuhrer simply wants to reunite all Germans. Is that such a bad thing?"

"Only when one is forced to serve a madman."

Aleksy's hand began to sweat around the knife he held. His legs were beginning to cramp as he leaned forward anticipating an attack. "Hurry it up, Danek!" he hissed into the shadows.

The guard was becoming angry now. "How dare you refer to the great Fuhrer as a madman!"

"Look, I know you're loyal to your leader just as I'm loyal to the work supervisor of this pig's sty - even if my loyalty is by obligation! Still, l have quotas to meet in dismantling your filthy Nazi uniforms. I cannot do it without all my men. And right now, one needs a doctor."

"That is your problem, pig!"

"But it is yours as well! One less man means less production, and you know it. Will you at least show a little mercy and take a look at this sick prisoner? I'd hate to report your indifference to your supervisor although a beating would no doubt turn *you* into a better prison guard."

The guard glared then stepped toward the closed gate, attempting to look in. Aleksy tensed as he heard the jangling of keys followed by metal connecting with metal. He could feel the sweat bead on his forehead. Every fiber within his body was alert and attentive as the key began to turn, then stopped.

"I refuse to open a cell door for such lowly dogs. Had you esteemed our great Fuhrer, perhaps there would have been reason to assist you. However, just to prove that I do have compassion, I'll call for a medical doctor…tomorrow."

The guard walked away; a smirk on his face.

Aleksy dropped his position in the shadows, rubbing tense muscles behind his neck. When Danek looked his way, Aleksy glared. "Fine escape artist you are," he said. "Perhaps next time you will esteem Hitler." The Polish boy retreated to his cot for the night.

After pondering their dilemma for the next several days, a new idea emerged. The prisoners determined they could use the knives provided for their labor to cut notches into the blades of some of the other knives. In turn, those knives would then be used to cut through the bars in the basement window from where their escape would take place.

The inmates got busy and were delighted to find that they were able to notch the knives as planned. However, they weren't prepared for what a slow process it would be to actually cut through the window bars. They determined it could take a week or more to do the job.

On a sticky summer morning, the teenage prisoners finally cut through the bottom bars running horizontally across the window. Next, they bent them outward and upward to provide an opening to freedom. One by one, the boys crawled through the window with Danek slipping behind the guard at the gate and expertly knocking him to the ground. He then hurried to join the others as they rushed toward the city streets where they split up and ran in several directions. The chaos of boys' boots slamming against rough pavement quickly drew attention. Having been instructed not to run toward the Swiss border, as this is where the guards would look first, the escapees scattered throughout the maze of streets. Aleksy, along with Danek and another boy decided to go east in the direction of Italy.

For three days, the three boys walked through the mountains. By the third day, their hunger drove them into a village where they helped an old lady rake hay in exchange for food.

Because it was Sunday, people were in the streets heading to church, including the village gendarme or police officer who immediately recognized the boys. Quick on his feet, the policeman captured the mortified Danek, but Aleksy was able to escape back into the mountains. As he ran against the flow of gathering citizens, he shouted out that something ahead had happened, and he didn't know exactly what. He smiled at the pursuers who ran past him, delighted by his clever antic. Meanwhile, the third boy in the trio of escapees had been caught, along with Danek, and returned to the prison.

A few days later, only Aleksy managed to remain free. Working quietly and efficiently, he stole bread and milk left by the milkman on the steps of houses as he continued south toward the Austrian-Italian border. However, ten days into his escape, the young Aleksy was finally captured by the German Air Force manning the border. He was immediately sent to the Gestapo who returned him to prison where all his comrades had once again been deposited. Only this time, he was put into a new cell, one that was filled with knee high water and a cement block on which to sleep. The huge water bugs and occasional rat didn't make it any easier, but Aleksy soon found they gave him good opportunity to think out loud as he conversed with them.

"Hello, you big rat," he sneered at the first sighting of an oversized rodent. "Did someone finally kill Hitler, and this is what he has become in the afterlife? Well, then, I will call you Adolf." Aleksy kicked the pest and sent him splashing into the water. Meanwhile, obese water bugs marched up the cement block to dry off, and the boy took delight in squishing them with his thumb. "So, I see Hitler's entire army has been put into prison as well. I always knew you were nothing but sleezy insects of which I must rid the world." Splat! Aleksy chuckled as he smashed another one.

For the next sixty days, the Polish boy lived in total darkness with a little bread and water to keep him alive. He allowed his mind to take him into the past as well as the future, but never the present. The present consisted of disgusting conditions and would only serve to depress him and possibly bring about his decline. Many prisoners of this very cell had been known to go over the edge; they would scream and beg to get out, but to no avail. Once they were freed, they were unable to do much of anything, their minds gone. Aleksy needed *his* mind and intended to keep it.

So, it was in this cell that Aleksy traveled to his childhood village, home to a carefree life of playing Juro Janosik with Koby, shooting their magical arrows as they robbed from the rich to give to the poor. He smiled as he envisioned Koby pushing him into the local swimming hole then pulverizing him in winter with the fastest snowballs in all of Europe. It was definitely memories of his friend that kept Aleksy sane during his days of lonely captivity. Wouldn't Koby be surprised, he wondered, to know that he had played a vital role in Aleksy's stability?

Then there were the daydreams of what was yet to come. He imagined leading an army that would wipe out all of Hitler's troops returning the European nations to their rightful owners. He'd make a point to visit each one after the war ended where he'd be welcomed as a hero. From there the boy would return home or maybe even go to America. He always wanted to visit the land of the free.

The odd part is that while Aleksy was alone in his cell he never *felt* alone. Was it the rats and water bugs that made him feel he had company? No, it was more like the presence of a person. Maybe it was the spirits of those who had suffered in this very cell, or even died while confined here. All he knew was that he felt peaceful and content, regardless of the conditions.

Even the guards found it odd that Aleksy had not once screamed or yelled out. He just seemed to take his confinement in stride, even to the point of being happy. Other than having lost several pounds, the ordeal had not left any obvious marks on him. The guards puzzled over this seemingly supernatural circumstance.

Following his punishment, Aleksy was returned to his original cell and to all the boys who had escaped with him. However, he was soon confronted by a very angry Gestapo who relayed that the Nazi police still wanted him to stand trial for possession of guns and the possible transfer of weapons to Poland. He was told that he would "lose his head" over this. The thoughts of decapitation were more than a man of any age could bear, but even less, a teenager. Aleksy shuddered, knowing it would take a miracle or a fast thinking mind to get him out of this jam. Not much on miracles at this point in his life, he opted for the latter.

Still, long before any master plan could be formulated, Aleksy found himself on trial locally for his recent escape from prison. As he sat through the proceedings, the local Gestapos did all they could to belittle him.

"He is a danger to Germany," stated one officer.

"He has no concern for the well-being of Germany even after being given the opportunity for adoption into this fine land."

"Hmph," thought Aleksy, "When was he ever offered adoption? Slavery perhaps, but certainly not adoption."

"He is nothing but a Polish pig," said another.

"A liar and a traitor."

And still the insults came as the German judge looked from one accuser to the next.

"He should be executed immediately!" declared another.

"By firing squad!"

"He's not good enough for such a privilege, hang him!"

"If we return him to his original jurisdiction to stand trial, he will be decapitated, a just punishment for his crimes against the fatherland."

"But that would be a reward – a quick death. Should he not suffer awhile for the trouble he has caused?"

"No! we need to make an example of him!"

Aleksy couldn't help but feel a little shaken at this point. He tried to stay calm by reminding himself that his luck had been good; the negative threats were only propaganda.

Finally, the insults stopped and the judge stared at him for what felt like several minutes before he spoke.

"Stand up, young man."

Aleksy stood. "Why did you commit such crimes against the fatherland when you were shown hospitality as an orphan?"

"This is not my fatherland, and I don't think slave labor is hospitality."

"You should show respect, young man, to the one who decides your fate."

"Yes sir." Aleksy dropped his head.

The Judge looked at the paperwork before him. "I see you're not quite eighteen years old yet."

Aleksy wasn't sure if this was a good thing or bad.

The judge continued. "If you were eighteen, I could easily have you hanged. But since you are not of age, I will show a little leniency and sentence you to hard labor instead until you can be transferred to stand trial for the charges on firing an unregistered weapon. The courts of your former jurisdiction will deal with that. " The man banged his gavel on the wood surface of his desk declaring he had nothing more to say.

Aleksy tried not to sigh his relief out loud. The thing about good luck, one just didn't know when or where it might turn up. And this was one of those times Aleksy hoped it might show up again.

Several days later, a prison guard banged on the doors of the cells and called out what sounded like to Aleksy his name. In response, Aleksy loudly banged on his own cell door so the guard could locate him. He was then informed that he was being transferred to a special Gestapo prison outside the city. The boy turned to the wall and put his clothes on while the guard waited. A prisoners' clothing was usually removed upon entry into a cell, regardless of whether or not he had an audience of other prisoners. Aleksy found the philosophy somewhat humorous. Not many people would attempt an escape naked. Still, Aleksy had grinned mischievously at the thought of himself running exposed through the streets of Germany or Austria with nothing to hinder his speed.

"Where am I going from there?" asked the boy as he finally turned to face the guard.

"I don't know," he replied in a Ukrainian accent. "And it's best not to ask questions."

Aleksy left the city with the guard and traveled with him for a half hour or so until they arrived at a place that looked like a factory. Once inside, the guard handed the prisoner over to an older SS sergeant who stared at him with hard, steely eyes before calling to another guard to put him in a cell.

Turning toward the warden, whom Aleksy recognized also as Ukrainian, he asked in German, "So, exactly what is this place? Is it a work camp?"

"And why would you think that?"

"Because I've been sentenced to hard labor," replied the prisoner. "Besides, I thought I was to be returned to my former jurisdiction to stand trial there."

The guard shrugged. "All I know is that this is the last stop for any prisoner. They will hang you here."

The cell door clanged loudly behind Aleksy as the guard walked away.

"How could this be? I can't be hanged! I'm not eighteen!" he shouted as he rattled the bars of his cell. Had he not been sentenced to hard labor? His eyes frantically searched the cell for any means of escape but found none. All he found were four wide-eyed prisoners staring back at him. What had happened to his lucky streak? Aleksy was now in need of more than good luck. He definitely needed a miracle, and he needed it soon.

Chapter 10
Rosaries and Miracles

At eighteen, Elise was well settled into American life. Although she still missed her home, school and her friends kept her busy. She had finally received a letter from her mother sadly reporting the death of her beloved grand-mère. Aunt Emma had cried with her, knowing the girl wished she could be with her mother at this time, but it just wasn't possible.

As was the custom of her faith, Elise took the city bus to the local Catholic church to light a candle for her deceased grandmother. She quietly stepped inside the ornate structure turning toward the basin of holy water. She dipped her finger into it then made the sign of the cross.

As Elise moved her eyes about the sanctuary, she couldn't help but feel she'd been there before although she knew she never had. The furnishings, the candles, the statues all reminded her of home. Born and raised in the Catholic church, she'd been only a twelve-year-old child when she'd gone through confirmation classes. She studied the beautiful stained glass windows and relived each Bible story they represented including the names of the saints adorning the church walls. It was all so different from the church she now attended with her aunt and uncle. A little city church, quaint and friendly but lacking in the formality of which she had been so accustomed.

As she stepped toward the aisle that led to the candle display, Elise knelt to confirm the presence of God then continued up the aisle and into a side wing where several candles where glowing. She stopped in front of the display long enough to search for some loose coins in her purse, then dropped them into a wooden box before reaching for a small votive and lighting it.

She held the candle toward Heaven, and whispered, "Dear Heavenly Father, please show your mercy to my dear grand-mère. I pray that she will spend little to no time in purgatory as she was a righteous woman who loved You. Thank You for her life and for allowing her to be my grand-mère. Please let Your light shine on her. Amen."

She set the candle on the table before her with the others that had been lit and watched the flickering light. "Oh, Grand-mère," she whispered. "I had so hoped to see you again one day." A single tear slid down her face.

Elise slipped into a nearby pew and reached into her purse where she pulled out the rosary she had brought from France. Known among Catholics for its miraculous powers and its many mysteries, the rosary held no importance at the church her aunt and uncle attended. They never mentioned rosaries, nor did she ever see any among the members, so she kept this one hidden. She didn't think her aunt or uncle would make a big issue out of it, but in light of their generosity, she wanted to respect their faith. She smiled as she ran her fingers through the blue glass beads. It had been a gift from her grand-mère on her fifth birthday. And although she would not be confirmed by the Catholic church for another seven years, her grandmother had patiently worked with her, teaching the child every "Hail Mary" and every "Glory Be" as well as the difficult Apostles Creed and the "Our Father" prayer. Once she had it down, she was able to recite each step in twenty minutes or so, something in which her grand-mère, her personal mentor, had taken great pride.

Now, Elise held each bead perfectly, reciting all the things her grand-mère had taught her. She did it as a memorial to a lady who had meant so much to her; this would be the last time she would take part in a ritual that was quickly slipping away. Feeling an unusual urgency, Elise finally dropped the beads into her lap and began to pray for everyone everywhere. She prayed for her mother at home in France, for her father somewhere on the battlefield, for this terrible war to end, for her aunt, uncle and friends on the American home-front and as silly as it might sound, for her future husband whoever or wherever he might be. She prayed God would keep him safe in wartime because it was God's plan for each of them - regardless of any so-called rosary miracles.

Chapter11

My Enemy, My Friend

Aleksy studied his four new cellmates. They, too, were all young, yet representing French, Belgium, Dutch and Czech nations. Still, it was in the German language in which they found a common bond, and since they spoke it according to Aleksy, "better than the Nazis," it was definitely the language of choice. As Aleksy listened to their stories, he discovered that all were condemned to die by hanging. Would he as well? The guard had sounded certain of it. Aleksy wasn't sure which method would be worse, but he knew that if he still stood the chance of being transported back to his original jurisdiction to stand trial there, he would possibly have time to plot an escape and avoid execution. If not, at least decapitation would be swift.

Still, an uncertain horror swept through him as he rationalized that the Germans had evidently opted to incarcerate him here rather than return him to the farmers' village. Was it possible that, along with his cellmates, he too actually awaited the more immediate death of a hangman's noose? It was a thought the boy would not entertain. He quickly explained to the other young men that he had been sentenced to hard labor and therefore must be in the wrong place. Two of the prisoners cut their eyes toward one another as if to say Aleksy was in denial.

While he could only depend on the information given him, he didn't know one hundred percent that a transport train even existed, but he had to find out. To remain here, without further investigation, could mean imminent death, and this was not a chance he was willing to take.

The boy immediately banged on the cell door bringing the Ukrainian sergeant back.

"What do you want?" came the impatient response in the Polish language this time.

Aleksy could not hide his surprise. "You are Polish-Ukrainian!"

The man did not respond.

"Why are you in the German army?"

"Is it not in everyone's best interest to serve the Third Reich?" he asked.

Aleksy looked at the guard in disbelief. "Not if you're a true patriot.

"And you consider *yourself* a true patriot?"

"I want to see the German sergeant!" demanded Aleksy. "And I want to see him now!"

"And I want to rise up and walk on air," came the sarcastic reply. "Who do you think you are that the Nazis will jump at your every whim?" With that he walked off, leaving Aleksy to wonder if he'd blown his opportunity.

However, a short time later, the same steely-eyed German sergeant who earlier had greeted Aleksy with only a hard look studied him from across his metal desk. He noted that the boy spoke with an East German accent.

"You speak excellent German," he said, "in spite of your accent."

"Thank you," replied Aleksy. "I'm actually from the north and was originally slated to return there, but the train was going in a different direction. So, they kept me in prison here simply to await the next train. Meanwhile, I was put on trial and now have been sentenced to hard labor until the transport comes, but this is a place of execution."

The sergeant tilted his head as he contemplated what the boy had just said. "There may have been a mix-up; they've been known to happen. Unfortunately, you'll have to see the captain before anything can be done," he finally said. "And he won't be here until morning."

"Well, it appears that all I can do is wait anyway. But I do need to get this straightened out."

"For tonight I will put you in another cell. This way you won't be confused with the other prisoners awaiting the death sentence."

Aleksy let out an audible sigh of relief causing the sergeant to smile. Afterall, the boy would still face execution, only by a different method.

When the SS captain arrived early the next day, the German sergeant led the prisoner to the captain's office. Remembering his manners in the presence of the man who could save Aleksy's neck from a noose, the boy greeted the officer with respect.

"Good morning, sir. I'm not sure what has happened, but I don't believe I'm supposed to be here. I understood that I was to be sentenced to hard labor while awaiting my transport.

The captain studied the young man then pulled a sheet of plain paper across his desk.

"What is your name?"

The officer wrote it down then thumbed through some paperwork; he reached for the phone and rang up the facility's prison personnel. After a short conversation, he slowly returned the receiver to its cradle as if contemplating what had been said. Aleksy held his breath, his heart standing still in the space of seconds that followed.

"There has definitely been a mistake," he said. Someone else was to have been brought here; his name is a lot like yours."

If ever there was a moment for a young Polish Catholic to make the sign of the cross, it was now, yet Aleksy refrained. Luck had simply turned up again. Of course it had been steeped in the young man's ability to think things out in a rational way. Wasn't it his *own* nerve and wit that had pulled him out of this tight spot? Yes, his intelligence and magnetic attraction to good luck had served him well once again.

"I will keep you in a separate cell," said the captain, "until the military transport comes for you. In the meantime, I want you to take care of my rabbits, and I want you to stay away from the Ukrainians; they are not to be trusted."

Aleksy could feel the relief wash over him. This position would be considered plush compared to other tasks he could have been assigned, to think nothing of the judge's sentencing of hard labor.

The next day, he was escorted outside where he was introduced to a row of rabbit cages. Aleksy cleaned each one noting that they housed a total of sixteen rabbits. And what beautiful rabbits they were. He recognized them as Angora, their fur long and exceptionally soft. “What would a military man want with these creatures, especially so many?” he wondered.

As he worked, he watched the four men he had been incarcerated with only the day before, being taken from their own dwelling in chains and led somewhere behind a wooden barrier. The SS captain emerged from his office and ordered the boy to return to his cell.

“What’s happening to them?” asked Aleksy.

“They’re being led to their execution.”

A chill passed through the boy. “It could have been…”

The captain paused briefly. “Yes, it could have been, but it’s not.”

“So, what is happening to them now?”

“Well, if you must know, as we speak, they are being led to the gallows behind that wooden fence. I’m not sure whether a military horse or truck will pull the rope. It often depends on what’s readily available. No worries, though, your acquaintances will be seated comfortably in their last moments. When the rope does its job, they’ll know nothing. Regardless, it will be quick and not too inhumane, considering the crimes committed.”

“Such as?”

“Why, treason against the fatherland. Is there any other crime these days?”

Did Aleksy detect a bit of sarcasm coming from the captain? Curious, but relieved, the young soldier was glad to return to his cell where his eyes wouldn’t be tempted by the mysteries behind the wooden fence. In spite of his escape from certain death, it was obvious to Aleksy that if the Nazis had decided it was too much trouble to transport the mistaken prisoner, they could have done as they pleased. In that case, one more young man would have swung from a rope that day. Because of the Nazis’ notoriety for inhumane treatment, including the inducement of fear, Aleksy could not help but wonder about the kindness of a certain SS captain who had assigned a teenage boy the task of simply caring for his rabbits.

Following the executions, the captain returned for the caretaker of his pets. He seemed to be in a talkative mood.

"I used to be the commander of a unit of foot soldiers in Russia," he said. "However, after being wounded, everything changed. I accepted the 'invitation' to join the SS, and after being released from the hospital I was assigned to this dismal place. Not much to my story as you can tell."

"I would like to say that I'm sorry for your wounds and your bad luck in life, but it would be a lie."

"How could I expect a Pole to show sympathy to a Nazi?"

"You know that I am Polish?"

"Hitler's Third Reich knows everything. Hitler is always watching. I hear you were in possession of a firearm and that you escaped from the kindnesses shown you by an East German farmer."

"I'm not sure being locked in a shed and acting as slave labor was much of a kindness."

"Compared to other things, it was indeed."

"Sir, can I be truthful?"

"By all means. It's not my job to analyze the things you say. That's the job of judges . I simply see that executions are carried out."

"And you raise rabbits."

The man laughed. "I get your point," he said. "How do bunnies and executions go together?"

Encouraged by the man's laughter, Aleksy smiled and nodded.

"Our Fuhrer is experimenting with the beautiful coats of Angora rabbits to bring greater comfort to his soldiers. He wants to use the fur to line Nazi uniforms and even underwear. I look forward to receiving mine as it will be warm and soft in the winter against my shivering tush."

Aleksy smiled again, this time envisioning the captain wearing a fur-covered uniform. "But who will shear them?" he asked.

"Don't worry; that job is not for you, but for a master shearer. We cannot risk damaging the fur as lining enough garments for an entire army will take tons of hair. Your job is to simply care for them. Feed them plenty of fresh vegetables and keep their cages clean. Also, if you notice that the heating units in their cages aren't working properly, do let me know. We can't have our bunnies getting cold noses." The man chuckled.

The whole thing seemed sick to Aleksy. People were starving and freezing throughout the country, and yet rabbits were living in luxury. It didn't make sense.

The conversation turned as the captain asked, "Now back to this thing of being truthful. What brought you to this end-of-the-road place?"

Aleksy poured out his entire story from his moments at Warsaw to landing in this current situation. He felt he could trust the man. As he spent the next few days with his new "friend," he began to understand the captain's own predicament.

The man had been proud to rise to the ranks of an officer of the Third Reich. But much to his sorrow, he was not called back to his original position upon his release from the hospital. Instead, he'd been assigned to the position of a policeman, which inwardly he detested. "I was never meant to be a simple constable, but my superiors must think otherwise," he sadly conceded.

During the day, the captain was the only German at the prison while the Ukranian sergeant headed up the night duty. The German hated the Ukrainians. For one thing, he believed they were stupid and another, he believed them to be traitors of their own country. Also, they spoke little to no German which complicated things for everyone.

Two weeks later, the captain informed Aleksy that the prison had called to report that the awaited transport would be passing through in a day or two, and prison personnel would soon call for him. What was inevitable had too quickly come.

Suddenly the captain looked at his young friend. "I have a plan that might work. I will tell them that I have found you to be of great assistance to me, especially in the Angora Project. I will tell them that you are a master with the rabbits and that I require your help if this project is to be successful and therefore, now is not the time for a transport. I will reschedule it for a later date."

Aleksy couldn't believe his ears, surprise stamped on his face as the officer studied him and waited expectantly. "Yes, Captain! I would very much like to stay here as long as possible. Being returned for trial means sure death, and I'm far from ready to die!"

The captain smiled. "OK. I will call them at the prison to schedule a later transport."

From this point on, a strong bond grew between the two men of opposite worlds. Opposites in age, rank and nationality, but in a bigger way, opposites in the sense that the two men were enemies. What or who could have ever brought these two unlikely people together and at a time when one was earmarked for death? Was it luck? Fate? Perhaps something bigger? Maybe even a miracle of God? Whatever it was, it went beyond human reasoning, beyond human comprehension, and yes, definitely beyond human intelligence, even if Aleksander Rostek could not see otherwise. He simply accepted his lucky life.

As their time together lengthened, the two men shared their lives and histories with one another, making good on the hours and minutes they had together. They traded war experiences as a Polish fighter and a German fighter. Aleksy found out that the captain was married and even had children and pets. How could such a kind and family-loving man arrange the executions of young men?

Aleksy began to feel that his friend handled his position by verbally and mentally washing his hands of any responsibility. Because he did not personally hang the prisoners, although he was ordered to do so, he was able to take a small step away from it. Perhaps it was an unperceived picture of one called Pontius Pilot who also washed his hands at the killing of Jesus Christ. Aleksy was well read and therefore, couldn't help but make the correlation. While Roman soldiers had carried out the dirty work of their own superiors, the captain carried out the orders of *his* superiors. It was the Ukrainians who did the foul work, though. Besides, the captain knew that if they survived the war, these

Ukrainian deserters would eventually be hanged for treason anyway. So, why not let *them* carry the blame?

Aleksy and the captain swore never to betray one another for the things they had so openly shared. In a time when no one could be trusted, when words were whispered in code and eyes lowered to the pavement, the promises between two enemies could easily be thrown to the wind. Perhaps these promises were sparked by the age-old philosophy of loving one's neighbor as himself – even in wartime.

It was the summer of 1943, and Aleksy was now eighteen - officially old enough to be legally hanged or decapitated. He was informed that his deadly transport would arrive in the fall. The captain was sorrowful but could do nothing more to keep him alive and in this particular prison. He had already put himself at much risk, but the one thing he would not do was order the execution of his young friend.

"Aleksy," he said, watching the boy lift up a huge rabbit and set it carefully on the ground, "I've analyzed the situation of how to keep you safe, and no matter how I look at it, I realize I cannot let you go free. But, if I have you moved to a concentration camp, you are more likely to live through the war. You are young and strong."

Aleksy listened intently as he wiped out the rabbit cage.

"When the transport soldiers arrive, I will tell them that officers came in and took you away for further questioning, and for some reason they've yet to return with you. I will tell them that possibly there was an execution as you were slated for it anyway. What do you think?"

Aleksy considered the plan. "Why can't you just let me go free, Captain? I feel that would be the easiest thing to do."

"I wish that were the case, but the authorities would be on us quicker than you could blink. And once you're recaptured, no more chances would be taken. It would mean your immediate death; I can't do that to you."

"Thank you, my friend," he replied, believing this man had shown more concern for him than his own father. "I trust your plan. Go ahead and transfer me to the concentration camp since it might give me a better chance for survival - as crazy as it sounds. Otherwise, all that awaits me is a guillotine. It's a no-brainer, Captain."

Both men knew the captain's plan was chancy and that regardless of the outcome, it would soon separate the two friends. But without taking this risk, both also knew Aleksy wouldn't survive. The Polish boy simply accepted the sacrifices made in the name of wartime friendship. Long or short lived, such friendship could never be fully comprehended. It went beyond intellectual understanding. He shrugged. Perhaps more than one Polish man would carry a world of debt in his heart because of a chance friendship with one beloved enemy. Yet this was something that remained to be seen, and for now, it had to be hidden away, possibly forever.

Chapter 12

The Dangers of Inmate Cuisine

It was the worst time of year to endure a concentration camp, but Aleksy wasn't going to look a gift horse in the mouth. Fall had arrived with an unusually brutal winter wind. Aleksy's captain friend had managed to keep the Pole through the summer before he was forced to send him away. Now aboard the transport truck filled with prisoners, Aleksy shivered as the vehicle rattled back and forth on the damaged German roads toward Camp Elsnig. Was it the cold that made him tremble or fear of the unknown? The boy laughed at his ridiculous thought. He'd proven many times that he was exceptionally brave.

As Aleksy and the others emerged from the truck, they were greeted by guns pointed toward their faces accompanied by the yelling of SS men. It was as if they were all angry. Aleksy hardly had a chance to get his bearings before he was pushed into a nearby "processing" building.

"Remove your slimy clothes!" barked a guard.

The teenager preceded to undo his shirt buttons, one by one. but the impatient guard grabbed hold of the garment and ripped it off. "Hurry up," he commanded. "A much larger transport is coming in, and I have no time to fool with you. But if I kill you, there will be one less filthy mouth to feed. So, move if you want to live!"

Aleksy quickly stepped from his trousers and grabbed the striped uniform thrown his way. He pulled the shirt over his head, catching the scent of mildew. It even felt damp. He stepped into the matching black and white bottoms then felt himself pushed along before he was even upright. From there, he was ushered into a room where he joined an assembly line of prisoners having their hair "masterfully" sheared. As the clippers slid across his head, Aleksy grimaced. He knew from the nicks the clipper made, his barber was far from professional. He ran his hand across the stubble on his freshly shaved head. "At least I still have a head," he grimaced, unaware that his fallen locks would be added to trillions of others woven into upholstery or Nazi uniforms.

The next stop was to affirm his identity and receive his numerical name now that he was a bona fide member of an official concentration camp, and no longer part of a prisoner of war camp. A red triangle cut from cloth marked him as a political prisoner, and Aleksy wore it with pride - it let the world know that he hated Nazi politics; forget that it was intended to be a mark of shame.

He soon found that his new "job" would involve digging drainage ditches then filling them with concrete pipes. The frigid air cut through him as he worked; his striped uniform didn't come with a coat. In order to survive, Aleksy knew he had to keep moving or hypothermia would set in. He didn't want to be the next stiff loaded onto the growing pile of bodies hauled to the incinerator - a secret they thought they kept hidden, but the disgusting odor gave them away.

That night, Aleksy found himself in a barrack full of Polish prisoners. While it was good to hear his mother tongue, it was also unnerving. He was determined to fly under the radar as much as possible. The less people knew about him, the better.

As he was about to enter his quarters for the night, Aleksy noticed the other prisoners stripping to their bare skin and handing their prison garb to a stone-faced sentry standing next to the door.

Aleksy leaned over and whispered to the inmate closest to him. "You've got to be kidding," he said. "It must be twenty below, even inside these barracks."

The man sighed, "It's their way to keep us submissive – and from escaping."

Aleksy chuckled softly, "I don't think too many would consider escaping in this frigid cold, even fully clothed."

He was rewarded with a toothless smile. "You'd be surprised what a man's mind will cause him to do. Stick around long enough, and you'll see."

"No thank you. If there's any chance to move on, I'm out of here."

The two men filed past the guard, handing him their clothing. He pointed to a corner bunk and told Aleksy he was to sleep there, then presented him with a crude piece of blanket, a scrap of coarse material. Aleksy wrapped it around the most personal parts of his body and headed to his new quarters, only to find he had company. Lots of company. His bunk was home to five other men.

They nodded, introducing themselves, all Poles. Each climbed onto the bottom bed staking his claim before Aleksy was allowed to choose his own spot. One had to respect tenure, though, and the teen knew he ranked at the bottom of this totem pole. Therefore, his task was fairly easy given the space available. He nestled into the thin layer of musty straw trying to get comfortable, then dozed restlessly through the night. As much as he tried to force himself to sleep, he'd suddenly awaken to the sound of snoring in his ear. Or worse yet, he'd awaken to find himself slapping at his legs as tiny critters feasted on fresh meat.

The next morning, Aleksy was given a small portion of bread for breakfast and a cup of strong coffee made from acorns. It was wartime, and prisoners didn't deserve the real stuff even if it was available.

Tempted to spit it out, he swallowed it with a gulp knowing any nourishment would be his ticket to freedom because nourishment was strength and strength was escape. So, he drained the cup, acorn grounds included.

As the months progressed, Aleksy would find that one of the worst parts of his ordeal at Elsnig was the bitter cold and lack of food. The prisoners worked from sun-up to sun-down with little relief from the elements. The liter of lunchtime soup did little to warm them as it was cold by the time they took their first slurp.

"What's in this stuff?" he asked an older man shivering next to him.

"It's more like what's *not* in this stuff, fella. But in case you can't tell, mainly water, cold water, boy, and if you're lucky, half a potato."

Suddenly, a shriek sounded among the diners. "I've got one! I've got one! A piece of cabbage," the happy voice called out. Aleksy recognized the voice as that of one of his bedmates.

Another prisoner jumped up. "Well, give it to me."

"Are you crazy? This is *my* prize!"

"No, *you're* the crazy one! I shared a quarter of a potato with you last week or have you forgotten?"

"Don't be ridiculous! There's not enough cabbage in this dirty water to amount to anything, much less share with anyone; there's just one leaf and it's mine!"

As Aleksy studied the conflict, he couldn't help but be amused. He dubbed one fella "Potato Man" and the other "Cabbage Head." He continued to watch the drama play out while sipping his own cold soup.

Potato Man jumped up splashing half his tasteless soup down his own shirt. Cabbage Head followed suit but first handed his cup to a man sitting next to him. Then the fight erupted. Aleksy wasn't sure what to make of it, so he kept his distance.

Suddenly a shot rang out, and Potato Man dropped to the frozen ground, blood oozing from his skull. The SS Guard motioned to Cabbage Head, "Drag him to the latrine with the others. You can pick him up on your way back from work duty."

Aleksy soon found out that the latrine served as an infirmary. Anyone found sick was stripped and placed there naked. By the time the work teams returned for supper, the sick would be long dead. The prisoners would then bury their comrades' hard, stiff bodies.

That night Aleksy slept a little better, probably because he was chilled to the bone and exhausted.

As he slumbered, he dreamed of people yelling and running in every direction. There were dogs barking and babies crying, then a gun went off. He jerked awake, calmed by the even snoring of two of his bunkmates. He flipped onto his side and smacked at something crawling beneath the cold, wet straw before returning to his sleep.

Little did the young man know that while he slept, someone continued the long night vigil of watching his every breath…and He had a plan for Aleksander Rostek.

Chapter 13

The Stench of Death

As the prisoners climbed from bed to begin their morning routine, they seemed more solemn than the day before. It didn't take Aleksy long to find out why. The gunfire that had sounded out in his dreams wasn't part of a dream after all. The Gestapo had made a visit in the night and disappeared with the man Aleksy had dubbed "Cabbage Head." The realization became clear as the boy found himself staring down on the man's lifeless body tossed into the latrine.

Aleksy tried to make sense of it. "Was a solitary cabbage leaf worth one's life?" he asked aloud, then shrugged. "Evidently so." He pulled the corpse toward the door and the waiting cart, already piled high with frozen bodies, wondering if anyone would even bother to mourn him.

"Not my problem," he mumbled, at yet another attempt to keep his own sanity in a world gone mad. "Moral of the story? Just don't let anyone know what's in your soup," he chuckled to himself then reached over and closed the eyelids of the naked dead man. "More room in my bunk tonight," he thought.

Aleksy found physical labor, although brutal at times, to be his friend. As he was already in decent health, the work load increased his muscle strength and flexibility; compared to other prisoners, he was in great shape. His main goal became that of acquiring enough food to keep his body fueled. On one work assignment, he spotted an unexpected food source – live pigs.

The Germans had a ready supply of squealing bacon at their disposal, live bacon that required food. Nightly, Aleksy would sneak to the pig pen where he would hide behind a stack of large barrels and watch as the kitchen personnel fed mouthwatering leftovers to the grunting swine. Once the coast was clear, he had all the food he could eat. The first time Aleksy watched this from his hiding place he became angry as he thought about so many prison inmates dying from hunger. Yet, he knew his own survival depended on discretion, and this was a secret he dared not share. Unfortunately, detection was eventually bound to happen.

As he'd done for weeks now, Aleksy tiptoed toward the now familiar pig trough, careful not to excite the large feasting pigs lest he become part of the meal. He leaned into the crib hastily filling his mouth with potatoes, corn and beans, oblivious to the odor and filth. Suddenly the backdoor to the kitchen banged open, and Aleksy found himself face to face with a German cook. Both men froze.

"What are you doing here?" bellowed the German.

"Feeding the pigs," Aleksy calmly replied.

The man paused a second as if sizing up what had just been said then burst into uproarious laughter.

"Hey, Heinz!" he yelled. " Get a load of this! A pig feeding a pig!"

The other man appeared at the kitchen door wiping his hands on a soiled dishcloth. He perused the scene, and an evil smile stretched across his face. "That sure is something you don't see every day." Then toward Aleksy, "So what are you feedin' those pigs, Pig Boy?"

"Half a potato or a piece of cabbage. Some days a little bread. Depends on what I'm being fed."

The first man looked at Heinz. "Well, now that's real nice of our guest, isn't it? Sharing his food with a bunch of hogs."

The taunting was beginning to get on Aleksy's last nerve, but he couldn't let them see that. He stood perfectly still as the rooting swine worked around him to devour their evening snack.

"Well, Pig Boy, since you like feeding your brothers, we'll be glad to let you help out with that. Anything to help us save a little work."

The two men laughed with one another. "Keep an eye on our visitor," said Heinz. "I'll be right back."

Aleksy stared straight ahead. If the German should return with a gun, he'd die proud for Poland, facing the enemy, even from a pig's sty. He grimaced. From that point it was a good possibility he would be feeding the pigs all right. The two Germans would no doubt think it hilarious for the swine to finish off his dead body.

Suddenly an SS man appeared, his rifle resting in its shoulder strap. He stepped toward the pig pen then stopped. "Come here, boy," he said, "I don't wish to muddy my boots."

Aleksy climbed from the pen and approached the guard who immediately slammed his fist into Aleksy's face. "Is *that* how you treat the hospitality of the Third Reich? Feeding your good food to the pigs? Do you know what it cost to keep you people fed?"

Aleksy continued to stare into the man's eyes as blood trickled from his nose and dripped off his chin.

"Well, then. If you like our pigs so much, you may sleep out here with them. Under no circumstances though, will you eat their food! Do you understand?"

"Yes, sir," he responded.

Heinz stepped from the kitchen door and approached the guard. "Sir, hopefully these will do." He displayed a roll of heavy duty rope and a long narrow towel for drying dishes.

The guard nodded. "Carry on," he said, moving to more important matters.

The two kitchen helpers preceded to tie Aleksy's hands behind his back, pulling the heavy rope so that it cut into his wrists and shot pain through his arms. Next, they pushed him to the ground and bound his feet so tightly he could feel the circulation leaving his legs.

Heinz and his friend then worked together to wrap the long kitchen towel through his mouth and around the back of his head where it was knotted in place. "So, you won't be tempted to eat the piggy's food," one of them smirked. Aleksy could taste the blood that dripped from his nose onto the cloth below nearly gagging him. At least he could still breathe.

Together the two men picked him up and hoisted the boy into the pen. "Oink, oink, oink," they harassed, then smacking one another on the back, turned toward the kitchen.

For the next week, Aleksy would spend his nights in the pig sty contemplating a story he had once heard of a young man who had gone into a far country and lived with the pigs after blowing his early inheritance. “Such a ridiculous fable,” he decided.

While being bound with heavy ropes wasn’t too comfortable, he finally learned to wiggle into a relaxed enough position to sleep on the hard earth. And once the pigs settled down, he found they provided more warmth on these frigid nights than four or five men piled together in one bed. Of course, any remnants of pig food did tend to draw rats, but they seemed content to stay in the trough lapping up whatever was left. For this, Aleksy was grateful as his tied-up limbs provided no way to fend off flesh-gnawing rodents.

Each morning the warden would come to the pig sty to release the prisoner to the normal cup of acorn coffee and stale, sometimes moldy, portion of bread. There were times Aleksy found himself coveting the scraps fed to the pigs. Finally, the punishment had run its course with the SS guard, and the boy was released back to the prisoners’ bunk.

~~~~~~~

Soon after, Aleksy was moved to a new camp, Camp Merseburg, where he and fellow prisoners worked near the Leunawerke compound. Here, employees were producing gas from coal for the war effort. It was also here that hundreds of prisoners were assigned to the backbreaking work of digging sand to build antiaircraft bunkers for the Germans. The prisoners were marched to the work site daily, a one-way trip of around four miles. And while Aleksy had strength that others did not, he found the eight mile hike wearing. It was all he could do to return to his camp at the end of the day where he and the others were treated to a supper far worse than anything he’d had since his ordeal began - potato peelings and murky water. Definitely, the pigs kept at Camp Elsnik had fared much better than these prisoners.

Aleksy’s job, along with a work team of several other men, was to uncover or abstract the sand that lay beneath the soil. A steam shovel would fill train cars with top soil then deliver it to
~~~~~~~

Aleksy's crew who would manually shovel the dirt from the cars then dig through it for the coveted sand needed to make concrete bunkers. Unfortunately, Aleksy nor his team could keep up with the demand as wagon after wagon arrived too quickly to abstract the dirt and efficiently sift through it. These poor workers gave new meaning to a "skeleton" crew as they were badly undernourished and severely weakened. Still, Aleksy pushed on, knowing it had come to survival of the fittest.

The men were guarded by an SS man named Nagel. He was a cruel taskmaster and would kill anyone who fell and couldn't get up or who didn't work fast enough. He seemed to delight in murdering pitiful, beaten down men. His method of murder was to chop the fallen victim's head with a spade by standing on it until decapitation occurred. Afterwards, he beckoned to three men who would pick up the deceased, two retrieved the body and one the head, then the headless man would be laid to rest just beneath the top soil. Common sense kept Aleksy as far away from him as possible.

One day, Nagel decided the work team needed a better plan when it came to removing the dirt from the train cars. He instructed four men at a time to lift the train from one side of the tracks then tip it over on its side so the dirt would fall out. While it may have been good in theory, it didn't work too well in practice. The rich top soil tended to stick to the insides of the car and the men were so weak it was a struggle to push the heavy container on its side. Of course, this didn't set well with Nagel.

He screamed at the men, knocking two within close range to the ground with the butt of his gun, then shooting them on the spot. Aleksy continued to keep his distance from this crazy man with a short temper. He preferred not to be his next target.

"Get over here!" he yelled at one prisoner sifting for sand. "Drag these dead men to the hole you're digging, and dump them in!"

The man quickly complied although dragging even emaciated bodies a few feet was a struggle. A trail of blood trickled through the sand behind him. No one dared help with the task for fear of being shot; one quickly learned to do only what

Nagel commanded. The prisoner buried the two bodies as capably as he could beneath the top soil then immediately began sifting through the dirt just as if it had never happened. Unfortunately, it wasn't the right thing to do.

"Hey, you!" Nagel yelled at him again. The man looked up at his overseer.

"Did I tell you to return to sifting sand?"

"N-no sir," he responded.

"Then why did you?" he asked, siting his gun.

"B-because we have a quota to meet for our blessed Fuhrer."

Nagel lowered his gun and smiled giving the Heil Hitler salute to which the prisoner responded.

Aleksy watched in amazement as sweat dropped from the prisoner's forehead and he returned to sifting for sand.

Nagle locked eyes with the boy who quickly returned to his own sifting lest he become the next victim of this insane maniac.

As the days trudged into the new year, Aleksy and his co-laborers continued to work from seven in the morning until six at night, stopping only for a half hour to partake of the allotted lunchtime nourishment—a small dish of watery soup containing little to no vegetable stock; it's taste was that of dirty dishwater.

There were times, Aleksy felt he would never escape his captivity, and in those moments, he thought of his captain friend who had done all he could to spare the boy's life. If not for him, Aleksy would have been long dead. "But is this truly living?" he wondered. "Is this of what my life is to consist?"

Aleksy knew he was there for a greater purpose than just existence. However, from where that revelation had come, he wasn't quite certain; still, he believed himself to be of heroic stock. And he was stubborn enough to believe that perhaps he was indeed indispensable. He smiled. "After all, for the past four years, I have made it against all odds; why can't I survive? Luck is on my side."

Six months later, while the prisoners methodically repeated the mindless task of shoveling sand, and burying comrades whom

Nagel continued to mow down, a single aircraft made a circle around the factory right before lunch and left. Within an hour or so, huge allied bombers, their white backwash ripping through the blue skies, hit the refinery with what seemed like thousands of bombs.

Although ten miles from the usual work area that day, Aleksy and his workmates witnessed smoke coming from the processing plant. Along with their guard, they stared in amazement at the blazing inferno. The prisoners were delighted at what they saw, yet Nagel was hysterical with fright, possibly due to the fact that his own house, along with those of the refinery workers, was located next to the factory.

The inmates sneered behind his back. Perhaps now he would get his just reward for the way he treated them. The men joked among themselves.

"Now *he* will see how it feels to be a victim," said one.

"Yes," agreed another, "I hope he returns home to find his 'castle' in a heap of rubble."

"And his old woman and children dead," piped up another.

Aleksy hardly cringed at the brutal comments. After all, hadn't they all become desensitized with so much death and killing surrounding them? It was all in a day's work.

Nagel watched the sky in obvious distress. The more distressed he appeared, the more the prisoners loved it. Still, they kept their distance from this Nazi time bomb.

Once the bombers had disappeared, a single aircraft flew around the blazing refinery dropping "Stars and Stripes" newspapers to the ground. Aleksy brazenly asked permission to retrieve a copy, to which Nagel replied, "I'll shoot you if you do."

Soon, though, the guard gave in to curiosity and allowed the boy to pick up the tabloid. Aleksy looked over his shoulder to make sure Nagel hadn't put him in the sites of his high-powered rifle. As he bent down to retrieve the sacred parchments, he noticed photos of German prisoners of war in the U.S. eating what appeared to be delicious food.

"Wouldn't you rather be in the US experiencing the good life rather than dealing with all the stresses of managing stupid prisoners?" asked Aleksy in the German dialect.

"I did not know that you speak German," came the surprised reply. "Besides, the photos are only propaganda."

"How can you be so sure?"

"Because it's wartime, you fool!" replied Nagel smacking Aleksy on the head. "And everybody lies in wartime!"

Aleksy rubbed his smarting head and continued to look at the newspaper, chuckling as he read a headline stating, "Your Leaders Are Crazy" by Sir Arthur Harris.

Nagel jerked it from his hand, "Give me that!"

Before the conversation could go further, a siren went off, summoning all prisoners to the now burning factory. There was work to be done, and labor was needed. From this point on, the detainees' job description changed. Instead of digging through soil for sand, they would now dig through the soil for the dead. Not only had many German factory workers been killed, many prisoners had been killed as well, and somebody had to clean it all up.

Aleksy's section of workers was assigned the task of digging graves and collecting body parts of some one hundred German girls who had worked in the refinery offices. Turning their work into play, the boys collected enough body parts to form a whole person, smirking inside as they matched the scattered trunks and limbs to recreate the young German girls. While painful for the German soldiers, the prisoners agreed that the Germans deserved what had happened.

Once the dead had been interned, the inmates were ordered to clean what was left of the bomb-ravished factory. Hundreds of German workers appeared on the scene and began to put the refinery back together, a sure sign of their Nazi determination.

It was soon decided it was time to relocate the prisoners to other concentration camps, but this time they'd travel on foot. There'd be no train rides or truck transportation, only the benefit of what strength the prisoners could muster. Aleksy and his comrades felt the marching would never end, especially when the sun beat down on them with its unforgiving heat.

While it was important to support one another, there was no denying that this inhumane march would result in a true test of endurance. Always on the lookout for anything edible, the inmates were often responsible for advancing their own death.

One night, they found themselves camping in a farmer's produce patch. Yet for some, this field of hope would become their field of death. The land consisted of an abundance of sugar beets, a mouth-watering sight to the malnourished prisoners.

"Be careful what you eat," warned the son of a Polish farmer. "Eat only the leaves or you will end up very sick."

Aleksy watched in horror as the hungry prisoners tore into the burgundy beets, gorging as if they had no sense.

"Here," said one man, handing him a huge clump of the yield. "It's good! Eat up!" Then the man bent his head to sink his teeth into the juicy morsel. Aleksy watched as rivers of red juice dripped off his chin.

When the men eventually began to grab their stomachs in pain and collapse in death, he was glad to have nibbled only on the leaves. Turning to the young Polish farmer he marveled, "I can't believe how they've dropped like flies!"

The Polish man shook his head. "They should have listened, but how do you convince a starving man not to eat the very food placed before him? It becomes a game of self-will and stamina."

"They've been far too hungry to listen to anything but their growling stomachs. Was there poison in the beets?"

"Only in the sense that their pitiful digestive systems could not handle it yet."

Aleksy responded with a sad smile, "Aside from the pain, perhaps they died happy."

"Yes, they deserved some kind of pleasure considering all they've been through."

Aleksy suddenly laughed. "We speak as if we're not a part of this nightmare, but on-lookers only."

The Polish farmer smiled. “Don’t worry, we’ll be reminded soon enough that it is our bad dream as well.”

The next morning, they were called to join the other survivors to help bury the dead. Then they fell into step again as the guards roused them on.

Aleksy was fortunate to soon find a way to quiet his constantly growling belly. As small rationings of food was often dispensed to the travelers to carry enroute, all Aleksy had to do was position himself behind a weaker man. Eventually the man dropped, unable to consume his food in the throws of death. Aleksy would be nearby to scavenge what was left. Of course, others had figured this out as well which could lead to great controversy.

One morning, Aleksy began the journey behind an Italian prisoner as he had observed that many of the Italians weren’t very strong and had become emaciated fairly quickly. And just as Aleksy expected, when the prisoner could take the marching conditions no longer, he fell into the road to breathe his last. On the ready, Aleksy reached for the small tin of rations that had fallen from the man’s pocket just as another inmate reached out to snatch up the coveted treasure.

“That’s mine,” firmly stated Aleksander Rostek.

“It’s just as much mine as yours,” retorted the Frenchman who had been following in Aleksy’s column of men.

A guard marching nearby motioned for them to hurry on. The inmates stepped over the dying man who was instantly shot and pulled to the side of the road. Aleksy knew that if the man was lucky in death, lagging prisoners would be commanded to bury him in a shallow grave by the road. Otherwise he would serve as a feast for scavengers picking up on the stench of death.

The two young men glared at one another, each determined in his own way.

“Give it to me!” demanded Aleksy.

The Frenchman sneered as he swallowed the stale bread ration right before Aleksy’s eyes, making the Polish man angry. He immediately shoved the Frenchman, getting the attention of the guard who had kept in step with the prisoners.

"What is this about?" he demanded.

"This man took my rations," Aleksy replied.

The Frenchman appeared rattled. "I d-did not," he stuttered.

"Then how do you explain the breadcrumbs on your dirty mouth?" asked the guard.

"I took them from a dead man."

At that, the guard began to beat him unmercifully with the butt of his gun. "How dare you rob from the dead!" he screamed.

The man threw his hands over his head, begging the guard to stop. "Please, don't! I have my own rations that I will give to another if you will just allow me to do so!"

The guard paused as the Frenchman fished his ration bag from within his uniform, then timidly held it toward Aleksy who reached out to take it." Immediately, the guard rendered a final crashing blow to the head of the admitted thief. Blood spattered in every direction as the man fell dead at Aleksy's feet. The Pole looked at the SS soldier in disbelief.

"Enjoy," the guard snickered before sauntering off.

Aleksy felt sick. He studied the coarse bread in the bag he held, then with a loss of appetite, dropped it on the road as he continued to march, never looking back but certain of the men who fell upon the crumbs behind him.

Chapter 14
Friends in Strange Places

As the winter turned to spring the men finally reached their destination stopping at a concentration camp in the northern part of Germany, Camp Neuengamme. There they were assigned the task of working on machines that produced some sort of metal pieces. While the work was not hard, the prisoners worked long hours. Still, Aleksy and his colleagues had the benefit of being inside and out of the elements which was considered good fortune. Aleksy also had the benefit of extra food for cleaning a guard's room each day. He didn't particularly care for the man, but the additional food portions he received proved to be enough to even share with his hungry friends. So, he quietly cleaned the German man's room never indicating that he spoke German. For reasons unknown even to himself, Aleksy chose to only speak the Polish language during this captivity. He was well aware that even faked ignorance could prove to be bliss.

As Aleksy labored daily in the large machine shop, the hours became an endless drudgery, an unending routine. He never knew how long he might be at one location, or if he'd ever find another opportunity for escape. Still, he knew he could not rush things; he considered himself a patient man which served him well in these unpredictable days.

Weeks became months, and the unsanitary conditions of prison life began to catch up with Aleksy. Insect bites and contaminated food had started to take a toll on his body, eventually leading to an infected abscess in his lower leg. The boy knew the hard knot had to be removed, but if he went to the factory doctor, his condition would be exposed, and if he were declared infirmed, he'd be put to death. Still, left unchecked, blood poison could build up in his body and eventually kill him anyway, he'd come too far to die from an infection.

Aleksy was delighted to find out from his Polish friends that a Polish doctor worked in the infirmary to assist with language translations and diagnosis. Aleksy immediately sought him out.

"This is serious," said the doctor as he examined the young Pole's leg. "How long have you known about this?"

"Three or four days."

"You should have to come to me sooner; blood poisoning can set in quickly and kill you."

"I didn't realize there was a Polish doctor. I'd rather die by blood poisoning than at the hands of a German."

"Well, Son, that risk is still there. The abscess must be removed, but you won't have an easy time of it because you'll still have to walk the two miles from the barracks each day to work. And if you can't do that, well...."

"Yes, I know," he replied. So much for encouragement from a doctor.

"I'll proceed with the extraction if you want to have it removed, but I must warn you that there is no anesthesia. We are given only a few bandages."

Aleksy nodded and lay back on the examining table.

"OK, doc. Still it's better to die at your hands than the hands of a Nazi."

The boy grimaced as he felt a dull blade puncture the skin of his leg. The pain was intense but Aleksy was a Polish soldier, not a cry baby. The doctor flushed it out with a little water then bandaged it with old strips of fabric that appeared to be the remnants of prisoner uniforms, probably those of his dead comrades.

He felt unsteady as the medic helped him off the table and to his feet. It hurt worse than the Pole would have expected. Still, he couldn't think about that as he had a two mile walk ahead of him.

The next morning, Aleksy managed to limp back to the factory and stand at his machine, expertly making production in spite of the pain ricocheting through his leg. But he knew he still needed fresh bandages and some type of numbing agent would be helpful, especially something to help fight infection. Meanwhile, his small ration of drinking water served as a cleansing agent.

At the end of the day, he reported to his second job of cleaning the German guard's room. There, he found a haven of useful supplies. First, he came across portions of an old newspaper strung about the room, pieces of which he stuck into his waistband for later use. Next, his eyes fell upon a bottle of fruit-flavored liquor, a popular drink among the Germans. While it's alcohol content was only 35% proof, it would serve nicely as an antiseptic. The boy smiled at his good luck.

Aleksy quickly checked the open doorway in case the guard should return. He knew he'd have to administer first aid right there as a missing alcohol bottle would be noticed, especially a full one. The boy scurried about the room looking for anything that could serve as a bandage and was pleased to find a small drawer filled with unmatched socks. He snatched up two and stuffed them into his pocket, then grabbed the bottle of liquor. Propping his foot onto the soldier's bed, Aleksy poured the substance over his wound gently rubbing the cool liquid in and watching it fester as infection met antiseptic. Then just as he was about to return the bottle to the man's dresser top, a voice spoke from behind him.

"So, I see you have discovered my liquor."

Still facing the chest of drawers, Aleksy did not move or speak. For all the German knew, the Pole could not understand a word he'd said.

The guard walked into the room and took the bottle from his hand. He smiled. "Yes, a man and his liquor. If he never drank before, this wretched war has given him good reason to do so."

He slowly removed the lid then inhaled deeply. "Ah, the aroma of alcohol. It can take you far away. It can take you home or even to new exotic places, and most importantly, it can take you away from this Hell hole." He turned the bottle up and drank deeply.

Aleksy slowly moved toward the door, taking advantage of the guard's reflective mood. As he reached the doorway, the man seemed to snap out of his daydreaming and scowled at Aleksy. "So, don't ever touch it again, or I will have to kill you! Can you understand that, Polish boy?"

Aleksy turned and hurried to his sleeping quarters, realizing he had not eaten the German guard's usual leftovers and that he had missed the prisoners' mealtime - not that he had missed much.

He climbed onto the top bunk and pulled the stolen socks from his pocket as well as the old newspaper pages from his waistband. Then carefully unfolding the doctor's bandage and studying the hole in his leg, he refolded the soiled paper dressing placing it back over the sore. Next, he tore off a square of newsprint which he formed into a small patch, and placed it over the doctor's covering giving extra padding to the now runny sore. He reached for a sock and pulled it onto his foot, smiling. As luck would have it, the sock fit snuggly holding the newsprint patch perfectly in place. "Ah, what good fortune," he thought. "As always, luck is with me."

Aleksy determinedly reported to his job each day as he tended to his leg with his meager supplies. He knew that to lay out would mean death by hanging or by lethal injection. After all, according to the Nazi's way of thinking, if one was too sick to work, then one certainly was too sick to live. Once it was determined that a prisoner was ill, a first aid member was summoned who quickly injected a special substance into the patient. One more corpse would then be loaded onto the burial cart. And Aleksy was determined that his dead body would not be one of them. So, he tended his wound religiously, never missing a day of work despite the pain. Eventually the wound healed, and the constant throbbing dissipated. Aleksy had beat the Germans again.

Because he had done such a good job of keeping silent in the presence of others, Aleksy's immediate supervisor, a German civilian, was surprised to eventually learn that his young charge spoke German. The supervisor even made it his goal to keep the SS officer from finding out and graciously kept Aleksy informed with news from the war front thereby, becoming a friend and advocate to the Polish boy.

"You won't have to put up with this mess much longer, Son," he assured him. "The allies are quickly progressing. That means the war should be a thing of the past soon."

Aleksy looked at him a bit skeptical. "Where did you hear such news?"

"From my friend who resides on the border of North Belgium. His city was easily over-taken by the allied forces; there wasn't even a fight."

"Ha," replied the boy, "fine military you Germans have."

His supervisor smiled. "Well, as much as I hate to admit it, it was some Polish armored division who did the deed."

"I'm not surprised Herr Supervisor. We are not made of the same yellow-bellied blood as German stock."

"So, then young friend, what do you know of this brave Polish army and the battle that took place with Poland?"

"All I really know is that our soldiers, young and old, are the most courageous men you will ever see on a battle field. I was only a fourteen-year-old child at the time everything erupted, caught up in the hateful aggression of your Adolf Hitler."

"Easy now," whispered the older man. "Ears and eyes are everywhere, listening and watching."

"Exactly! That is why I would not tell you about the Polish army even if I did know anything. You are probably Hitler's greatest advocate."

Aleksy's German supervisor chuckled. "Think what you will, young man, but trust me when I say help is on the way. I, too, am sick of this disgusting war."

"At least I have finally heard a German call it disgusting."

"Just don't let the SS know of our conversation, or we'll be put before the same firing squad."

"Don't worry, Sir. I delight too much in the idea of you standing before a *Polish* firing squad when this mess is over."

The supervisor grunted.

Aleksy grinned as he returned to his work.

The young Pole began to notice an air of fear among the German civilians who worked within the factory. Maybe the

German supervisor did know something. Still, the SS men were confident more German armies would come to their aid and thwart any attempts made by the allies to overthrow their military. Such were the false securities of Hitler's finest. They lived in a make-believe world according to Aleksy.

The morning of April, 1, 1945 arrived, and the prisoners were awakened early and put into marching processions. Any thought of an April Fool's Day joke was quickly dismissed as the sick were loaded into nearby empty railroad cars. Aleksy watched in horror as the Nazis locked down the trains and then proceeded to spray the wagons with gas sending the entire line of boxcars up in a blazing inferno muffling out the screams of the dying. The barracks the prisoners had just evacuated were set on fire as well. The remaining evacuated prisoners silently watched wondering what was in store for them and knowing they'd be surprised by nothing the Nazis did.

The prisoners waited as an order was read from Heinrich Himmler, head of the German Gestapo and SS, addressing the troops. He commanded the Germans not to give up the prisoners to the allied enemies, mainly political prisoners of which Aleksy had long been classified. He still wore the red triangle that branded him as such. The prisoners, now totaling a few hundred men, were then marched away from the advancing allies through small narrow back roads which proved to be a challenge for the less able-bodied souls of the group.

Prisoners who could not keep up on the 120-mile hike collapsed, thus ending their own lives as a bullet penetrated flesh and organs. Still, the marchers continued on their way with no time or even desire to pay last respects to the dead, who were stripped naked and left in ditches. So much for any hope of rescue. Had Aleksy's supervisor confused his facts?

This time the marchers traveled with little hope of food, sleeping on farmland as they moved closer toward yet at another camp - Camp Sandbostel. It was obvious that the point of the march had been to kill as many prisoners as possible. Upon their arrival 17 days later and with only 38 remaining prisoners out of more than 400, the Germans, no doubt, were feeling quite successful. Upon arrival at the camp, whatever previous atrocities the prisoners had already faced, Aleksy and his fellow inmates weren't prepared for what they would now see.

The barracks were full of the dead. Meanwhile, the living dead were found cooking human hearts over an open fire and eating them. Human corpses with holes in their chest cavities attested to their once life-giving organ. Aleksy and a newly formed band of friends stared in horror, one even vomiting up his partially empty stomach. The stench of evil far outweighed the stench of death itself.

This group of spectators, consisting of several boys of varying nationalities had over time migrated together. As Aleksy had observed them enduring long marches and strenuous work assignments, he determined that their combined youthful strength could help him survive, even help one another survive. Aleksy had become their unofficial leader, and now without words, they had formed a group that would back one another to the end.

This odd assortment of French, Belgian, Dutch, Polish, and Italian boys set up a night watch in which some of them would sleep, and the others would set guard armed with pieces of wooden sticks. Their would-be attackers consisted of a wide array of personalities: shell-shocked, gypsies, homosexuals, and criminals, to name a few, a multitude of people gone mad. It appeared they had been left to their own devices without so much as an officer anywhere within the terrifying compound. When it came to survival, each man was on his own.

The next day, the boys were filled with curiosity when they noticed a young SS man with a rifle standing in the middle of the camp. This was somewhat strange considering that no other SS guards were inside the fenced area, and none ever came into the compound alone perchance they be brutally attacked by the prisoners.

Aleksy pointed him out to his comrades, commenting that the soldier seemed a bit uptight. The boys watched as he held his rifle at the ready, slowly turning his head in every direction lest he be attacked from behind. "Why in the world has he entered the gates of this place?" asked Aleksy. "Doesn't he know his very life is considered nothing by these dying and delirious prisoners? They would love to rip his Nazi heart out and swallow it whole."

"Perhaps he has been ordered to stand there," suggested one of the friends.

"Maybe he is being punished," offered another.

"I would rather spend the rest of my military career peeling rotten potatoes and eating the smelly dirty peelings that fall on the floor than face this," said a young Frenchman.

The first boy responded with a sheepish grin, "Only because you are related to the cowardly Irish who have gotten off with a declaration of neutrality."

"I beg your pardon," he quipped. "I'm a red-blooded Frenchman through and through. I can't help that I like potatoes."

"We all like potatoes these days," responded a Pole, "even the peelings."

Throughout their nonsense, Aleksy studied the nervous SS man who now seemed to be sizing them up. For all the German knew, any of these prisoners could easily stage an uprising and kill him.

"I'm going to talk with him now," stated Aleksy. "Maybe we can help one another." The boys nodded in agreement, but warily watched their friend as he neared the armed SS guard.

"May I speak with you?" he asked in German.

"You're a German?" the guard responded nervously toying with the trigger of his loaded gun. Nervous and angry Germans were to be feared the most as they were potentially explosive.

"No," responded Aleksy. "I'm Polish, but my friends are from many other countries.

The German nodded.

"Why are you inside the camp? Isn't this rather foolish knowing the prisoners here would love to murder you?"

"I'm well aware of that," he responded tightening his grip on the gun. "I'm being punished for returning late from a pass; I'm required to stand guard alone in this camp during the day."

Aleksy returned to his waiting friends with this information and a plan. "I'm going to ask him if he would take me to the Polish officers' barracks where there is better treatment. The Polish typically look out for their own, so my nationality will be a plus; perhaps they will give me food." The boys excitedly agreed over the prospect of quieting their empty stomachs.

The next day, Aleksy once again approached the soldier, whose name he eventually learned was Schmid. He laid out his idea for visiting the Polish officers and possibly acquiring food. Schmid studied the daring young Aleksy and then rubbing his chin, admitted that he would definitely be interested in helping. Perhaps these prisoners would be a help to him in return if he were ever attacked. Still there was one problem: a German soldier who knew of Schmid's punishment stood at the entrance to the officers' quarters. He'd no doubt shoot Schmid for treason.

"The Polish officers have cigarettes they'd surely be willing to share with you German soldiers for letting us see them," replied Aleksy. "Is it not worth a try?" he asked appealing to the German boy's craving for nicotine.

Finally agreeing with this strategy, Schmid led the young prisoner to the officers' quarters from where he acquired not only cooked vegetables and bread, but cigarettes for both Schmid and the other German guard. Prisoners and guards were both well satisfied and began to see Aleksy as the hero he believed himself to be.

However, it didn't take long for the lack of food to quickly become a secondary concern as tensions among the prisoners escalated daily. During the night, a number of murders were committed by the criminal prisoners. The idea of a conscience by now was foreign to seasoned killers who lived here. Polish officers were removed from the camp in the name of safety, thereby, ending the food supply.

Two days later, Schmid called to Aleksy and shared with him that late that day the SS would be taking some German prisoners from the camp. It looked as if he would be serving as one of the escorts.

"If you and your comrades want to leave with me, I'll come for you when we're ready to begin the transport," he said in a quiet voice. "Remove the red triangles from your clothing as no records are being kept. I'll take you to the German barraks so the soldiers will simply think you're German political prisoners. You'll be able to walk out with them, then sneak to freedom."

Early in the evening, as instructed, the boys removed their cloth triangles and approached the German barracks with Schmid's help. Odd, but there seemed to be an abundance of German prisoners. Schmid, along with other SS soldiers formed the several hundred men and boys into four marching columns, and it was within this organized structure that the men finally began to move toward their next destination.

Schmid looked around then fell into step beside Aleksy. "We might get separated along the way," he said, "but if I'm anywhere near, I will cover for you and your friends. When you have the opportunity to run, run like crazy but be aware that the soldiers will shoot to kill. Take cover wherever you can." Aleksy nodded as Schmid moved on, wondering if he'd ever see him again. In spite of the Germans' hatred of their enemies, some had certainly proven to be friends in strange places.

Meanwhile, several of the German political prisoners showed signs of wearing down as their tired and frail legs dragged through the dirt slowing the marchers down. The guards took note and announced that those who were unable to walk should step out of the moving columns. Aleksy and his friends watched close to fifty people heed the call. They were instructed to sit down, and Aleksy could see the relief in their eyes at the sound of a truck approaching from the distance. "Well," thought the Polish lad, "perhaps the Nazis do have a little feeling for their own German citizens."

Meanwhile, the marching columns proceeded forward to the sound of machine gun fire as the trusting few were mowed down in cold blood, ridding the Nazis of further delay. The dead bodies were then unceremoniously tossed into the back of the military truck. Aleksy caught the eyes of one of his comrades as if to say, "Aren't we lucky we still have physical strength?" The stale and moldy rations they had been forced to consume were now paying off; they had been worth choking down after all.

The next morning, the assembly arrived at a railroad station at which the prisoners were instructed to board boxcars awaiting them. Menacing-looking anti-aircraft guns were attached to the front and the back of the train. The men were packed inside like animals with no possibility or hope for escape even if the opportunity presented itself. Packed tightly together in standing position, the claustrophobic didn't stand a chance, especially once the doors were nailed shut.

Aleksy felt the train lurch forward as he and his buddies fell into one another. Under no circumstances would this be a pleasant ride. If anything, it would be a journey deeper into the portals of Hell. The press of the crowd was the only thing that kept the prisoners from falling to the car's floor as they endured the rough, swaying ride that took them into the unknown. And then, the attack occurred.

The train stopped immediately as the allies fired AA guns and dropped bombs from above, never suspecting that the armed enemy train's cargo consisted of war time prisoners and civilians. The screaming of people trapped inside the cars ricocheted off the walls as their blood red-washed the interior of the train. The sound of people dying was a sound that would haunt Alexy forever.

In the mass confusion, the boy lost track of his friends, but miraculously was able to crawl from beneath a pile of bloody bodies through an opening left by a falling boxcar door. As the arid atmosphere filled his very being, Aleksy slid beneath one of the cars and behind one of the train's wheels. It was flimsy protection at best but all he could do for now while the ammo continued to fall. Then the inevitable occurred - Aleksy was hit.

Through excruciating pain, the boy waited behind the wheel listening as the last of the artillery dropped. Although he had lost much blood, he fought to stay alert refusing to be buried in a German's mass grave. Wrapping both hands around his injured leg, Aleksy could feel the rhythm of his pulsating heart beating against his blood-soaked hands. As gruesome as the sensation was, Aleksy knew it was his connection to life and he determined to maintain consciousness. He rolled over on his back and hugged his knees to his chest while listening for the dying sound of retreating enemy planes. Red hot pain speared through his upper leg.

In the eerie silence that followed, all that could be heard was the raspy breathing of a lone survivor. Aleksy slowly rolled back onto his stomach and cautiously peered around the wheel of the train looking for signs of German soldiers but saw none.

He smiled at his luck as he lay beneath the train, drops of blood dripping onto him from the cracks in the floor above. He thought about the dead that obviously surrounded him; there must have been some reason that he survived and they did not. "Polish luck," he whispered somewhat in awe.

Still, there remained the simple yet profound truth, "It is appointed once unto man to die." And for reasons unknown, this truly was not Aleksander Rostek's appointed time. A mysterious watcher continued to hold *that* clock as it ticked and ticked and ticked...

Chapter 15
To Dream a Little

Elise glanced at the clock in front of the classroom. Time was ticking away, and she still had to translate a short hand memo. She pressed the eraser end of her pencil into her bottom lip as she mentally read through the dots and squiggles before her. It was a good thing she had mastered the English language, or she'd never be able to make it as a secretary. Just as she signed her name to the translation with a flourish, the bell rang.

"OK, class," said the smiling teacher, "please stack your test questions and answer sheet on the front of my desk as you leave. You'll know your grade on Monday. Now, have a good weekend."

Elise gathered up her books, bid her teacher farewell and headed out the door where she practically bumped into Mildred. "Oh, Mid," she exclaimed, " I'm sorry! I guess I was so relieved to finish my test, I didn't watch where I was going."

"It's ok," replied her friend. "So, how do you think you did?"

"Actually, I felt pretty good about it. I want to do well, you know, because I'll stand a greater chance of Mrs. Tillon's recommendation for any secretarial openings once school is out."

"What about secretarial school?" asked her friend.

"That's not *even* in the budget," she sighed.

"Who knows? Maybe things will get better soon. You know there's talk that the war could be coming to an end soon."

"There's always 'talk' Mid, but nothing to back it. Anyway, have you given anymore thought to cosmetology school?"

"Oh, yeah! Lots of thoughts, but like you, I don't see it in the budget either. Plus, Mom and Dad have my little brothers and sisters to think of and well…it just hasn't been easy."

"Well, let's talk about something positive," quickly responded Elise, changing the subject. "Are you and Merle going to the USO tonight?"

"I think Merle is, but not me."

"Let me guess, you have another date with Jake and…"

"And you know how he hates to dance," ended Mildred with a frown.

Elise laughed. "And I know how your feet are always twitching to hit the dance floor."

"Yep, and it's been hard to tame these poor puppies. They start tapping away at the sound of a note, off key or on key."

"That first night I saw Jake out on the floor, I would have never dreamed he wasn't a dancer."

"That's just because you were so enthralled with your *own* sailor boy. If you'd looked a little closer, you would've seen all the scuff marks on the toes of my Mary Jane pumps."

Elise laughed. "Well, I won't be dancing tonight either. I took the night off as a junior hostess. Willie goes to sea again next week so, we wanted to spend some quality time together."

"It's only been a few weeks, Elise. Don't you think it's getting serious too fast?"

"You're a fine one to talk, Mid! You've seen Jake every single weekend yourself. And besides, I do believe there is such a thing as love at first sight, don't you?"

"Possibly, but that's because you read so many romance novels," Mildred jabbed back with a smile. "And then there's all those silly fashion magazines."

"And who reads them when I'm done?" quipped Elise with raised eyebrows.

"Ok, ok, enough said. So, where are you and Willie going for your quality time tonight?"

"Well, Aunt Emma suggested cooking dinner for us, and then we'll probably take a walk in the park and just talk, you know, dream a little."

Mildred shook her head, "Just don't let those dreams get away with you Elise. I wouldn't want you to get hurt."

Elise watched her friend disappear into the crowd of students heading out the door. "Well," she thought, "as if *that* didn't hurt." Oh well, what did her friends know about true love anyway? And didn't she pray that God would lead her to the one she would marry? She wondered if her friends even thought to pray for such things. Perhaps her own formal Catholic upbringing had been stronger than that of her Protestant friends. Of course, she was now fully immersed and she had to admit that it was her friends' ways, or rather God's ways, that had brought her to the truth, made her reconsider the foundation she'd been given in France.

Elise sighed as she unloaded her books into her locker. It looked as if God was keeping Willie safe throughout the war, and hadn't he brought them together at the USO? So why did she feel this constant urging to pray?

Chapter 16

Friendly Fire and Unfriendly Wounds

Aleksy knew he needed to create a tourniquet from his shirt which would require sitting up. He painfully crawled from under the train and onto a nearby road. By then he was gasping in unbearable agony as he tried to hold the gaping wound closed. It had picked up dirt and brush as he pushed himself toward a fallen tree on which to rest. Bit by bit, he finally reached it then gasped in surprise as he came face to face with a German soldier lying on the other side. Suddenly realizing that he still wore his prison uniform, Aleksy braced himself for the shots that were sure to come.

The soldier who held his gun in position lowered the barrel, but Aleksy had already dropped his face into his arms. “No need to take cover,” he consoled. “I’m not intending to put you through any more than you’ve already encountered.”

Carefully raising his head, Aleksy looked at the young German lying against the backside of the fallen tree. The man’s right shoulder was steeped in blood but tied off with a make-shift bandage.

“Sir,” Aleksy asked as he painfully tried to sit up. “Could you possibly help me bandage my leg?”

The soldier grimaced, whether in pain from his own injury or from the sight of the boy’s severely wounded limb, one couldn’t be certain. “Yeah, I’ll help you,” he consented.

He knelt on the side of the road using one hand and Aleksy’s assistance to tear the undamaged sleeve from his good arm. Together, the two created a temporary tourniquet around Aleksy’s leg. Then, shoulder-to-shoulder, they began a mile long trek toward a distant farm house, where upon arrival, they found no one home.

Thus, began a search for any and all first-aid supplies. The unsuspecting owners donated white linens to act as bandages.

Next, the young men were delighted beyond measure when the German exposed a cache of Polish and Russian vodka hidden deep within a cupboard.

Together they popped the corks raising their bottles in celebration that they were still alive. "To Germany!" declared the soldier raising his bottle high.

"And to Polish vodka," Aleksy dared to say as he too, raised his own bottle, a huge grin spreading across his face.

They drank deep to ease the pain of their injuries. Knowing full well they had to keep their heads about them, the men used the remaining contents to douse their wounds against infection. Once everything was back in place, and Aleksy had been assisted to a shady spot next to the road, the soldier took leave reassuring the Polish man that once he reached the nearby village he would send help back to his new friend. All the while, the German believing he was simply helping another German who happened to be a political prisoner of war.

A good while later, a horse-driven cart bearing a sign for the Red Cross rambled toward him. The Germans on board stopped and quickly jumped out saying that a soldier had reported Aleksy's location and his injuries. They had come as quickly as they could. Upon inspecting the wound, they shook their heads.

"You will need to go to the Red Cross station with us as you do not want the possibility of infection. This is a very bad injury, and you wouldn't want to risk losing your leg, would you?"

Aleksy shook his head back and forth. No, he would need that leg to eventually get out of Germany, of which he was quickly tiring.

The trio reached their destination in an hour where a German military doctor was moved to action upon seeing the fresh injury.

"Move a table next to the window," he instructed the soldiers. After hoisting the lad onto the table, he examined the wound. "Boy, you are quite the lucky one," he said.

"Yes sir," responded the patient. "I always have a way with luck."

"Good thing you do because you're carrying a live aircraft canon bullet in your leg."

Turning back to the soldiers he instructed them to open the window. "You seem to be in strong enough shape despite this wound," he continued. "However, you'll need to be extra strong for what I'm about to do. My plan is to cut into your leg and gently remove this ticking time bomb. If the bullet explodes, we are both dead. If it doesn't explode, well, you truly are a man of good luck."

The boy bit into a rag wishing he had another bottle of good Polish vodka to deaden the pain that would come. He closed his eyes and braced himself. Aleksy could feel the knife slicing into his skin and the doctor's nimble fingers probing for the bullet. Did it not seem to go much deeper than when the Polish prison doctor had cut into his absess? He held onto the sides of the table while the "surgeon" carefully reached into the opening and pulled out the instrument intended for death, a 20mm canon shell. Then without so much as a breath, he hurriedly threw it out the opened window where it promptly exploded, scattering its' deadly shrapnel into both the earth and sky.

Aleksy locked eyes with those of the doctor, smiling in spite of his pain. The doctor laughed and patted Aleksy's shoulder. "We did it," he cried out while dancing a jig. Once again the Polish boy had beat out death. His luck never seemed to run out.

As Aleksy lay recuperating, additional wounded boys and men came to the station, including some of his former comrades. And although he found it hard to believe, in came a German transport carrying the SS soldier, Schmid, into the infirmary.

"Schmid!" called out Aleksy. "You made it! You weren't killed in the train attack!"

Schmid looked at Aleksy, then grinned.

"What happened to you?" asked the Pole.

"Shot by friendly fire, at least that's what they tell me."

"Me too, only the allies had no idea; they thought they were firing on their enemies, not a train load of pitiful prisoners. Were you on that train too?" asked Aleksy.

"Of course not! I was in a military vehicle when the attack occurred. You wouldn't have believed the people running in every direction. I was ordered to shoot anything that moved."

Realization sunk in as Aleksy stared at Schmid. Schmid had defied the order. Not only was he willing to spare the lives of the boys he'd help escape, but the lives of others as well.

"I thought they wouldn't notice," he whispered, "since I aimed and shot over their heads. Anyway, I got it in the back."

Aleksy blinked. Was this man a coward or a friend? A patriot or a traitor? To his country, he was a traitor but to Aleksy, well, it appeared he had indeed been a friend.

"What will happen after you leave here?"

"Well, for one thing, I doubt I'll ever be able to walk out of this place. I'm told I'll be court marshalled for acts of treason. And then, if I'm lucky, I'll face execution. It has to be a lot easier than being labeled a coward the rest of my life." He turned his head toward the ceiling, "Those men had families, Aleksy. Mothers, wives and children. They deserve to go home, too, you know."

Aleksy tried to turn this over in his mind, especially the part about luck. How could being executed be considered good luck? He felt bad for his friend, and it was in this moment that Aleksy realized just how much he truly hated war. How could his father have ever been so energized by it?

As more wounded came in, Aleksy spotted a small Italian boy by the name of Pietro whom he had befriended as part of the group in the POW camp. The poor boy screamed out in pain continuously; he'd been shot in the gut, and it was a wonder he was still alive. Aleksy asked the doctor if there was anything at all to give the man, perhaps enough liquor to knock him out for awhile. The doctor said he'd see what he could do. A little later the boy quieted down and the other patients were able to get some rest. One by one, new arrivals were put into beds and assured by the doctor that he would take good care of them until the allied troops came through. However, this was not to be the case.

After midnight, the Gestapo suddenly appeared with heavy footsteps and guns aimed to shoot if necessary. They brutally piled the wounded on a truck where they were carted to a harbor and loaded onto a small freighter pirated by Hitler's infamous organization, the Schutzstaffe. There, the wounded were left on deck. Those not injured were ordered below to endure the transport.

"What's going on?" Aleksy called out to a German sailor.

"We don't know," he responded, approaching the wounded prisoner. "Just that we have been over-taken by what appear to be Hitler's Nazi troops."

"Where did all these Germans come from anyway? Weren't they all killed by the allied air strikes?"

The sailor threw out his hands and shrugged, "All I can tell you is that they came aboard in the night out of nowhere and demanded our weapons as well as the freighter."

"It's obvious that they have their own arsenal," remarked Aleksy sizing up the heavy artillery being moved about the deck. "There must be 2,000 prisoners on this thing."

"Actually, there may be more. The cargo area is stuffed with men. You are much better off up here even in the heat because you get a breeze occasionally to carry away the putrid odors of the sick and dying. Below, you can suffocate on the stench of vomit and bowel excretions alone. Be glad you are wounded. Otherwise you would be trapped in a tomb of filth."

Aleksy shuddered, "Do you think they plan to sink us in the middle of the ocean somewhere?"

"Whatever Hitler orders is what the Schutzstaffe does," replied the sailor.

"One fine ending for a patriot," thought Aleksy. Shark bait was not how he wanted to be remembered, "Hmph, as if anyone would remember me, anyway. No one even knows I exist, not even my own mother."

He gave a sad smile, and for a quick moment, saw himself looking into a little brown camera as his dad peeped from behind the picture-taking box. "I wonder if *he* even remembers me, and if he would be proud of me now?" Aleksy suddenly felt afraid. Was it possible to die and no one care or even remember? He turned his head to the side just as a breeze or *something* softly brushed against his face - a breeze that felt like gentle fingers.

Chapter 17
True Blue

Elise laughed at her friends as they continued to swoon over the handsome Cary Grant. You would think they were going to marry him. Besides, she had her eyes on Willie who was stationed at the Brooklyn Navy Yard. And he had his eye on her. She couldn't quite put her finger on it, but Elise loved seeing a man in uniform! Besides, at the ripe old age of forty, Cary Grant was far too old for her – and for her silly girlfriends, even if they refused to believe it.

Elise laughed along with twins Merle and Mildred over the antics of the comedy they'd just seen. Anything bearing a title like *Arsenic and Old Lace*, couldn't be too serious.

Merle put her hand over her crimson colored lips and giggled uncontrollably. "Can you believe how Cary reacted when he realized those two old ladies had killed that man? I thought I would die laughing, especially when he found out they had eleven other stiffs in the basement!"

"I wouldn't call all that snortin' 'laughing'," Mildred responded. " Mama would have had a fit to think you were gulping down air like that! Where did you get your manners, Merle? In a barn?"

"Well, it was funny, and you know it!"

"Now, now girls," chimed in Ruth, fixer of all problems. "The whole thing was hilarious! And it was such a nice escape from all this war stuff!"

The girls nodded in agreement as they returned to reality.

"Yes," said Elise, in her odd combination of a French and New York City accent. "I just wish this war would end so Willie could stay home and marry me."

"Oh, little French bird," said Mildred shaking her thick dark hair, "don't you know that he's got a girl in every port?"

"Maybe other sailors, but not my Willie! He's true blue!"

The girls linked arms as they marched across 50th West toward Times Square.

"We're just glad 'Mr. True Blue' had to work today. It's been far too long since we've had a girls' day out," declared Ruth.

The other three friends nodded. "It's this crazy war," Elise responded.

"You can say that again," agreed Merle. "I'm tired of eyeliner smearing all over the backs of my legs. I miss my nylons!"

"Well, if you weren't so cheap and bought a better cosmetic brand, it would help. Besides, I don't know why you even feel the need to put those ridiculous black lines up the backs of your legs anyway."

"What? And have people think I'm not wearing nylons? Why I'd feel half dressed!"

"You are half dressed, Merle - just like everybody else; nobody has nylons because our soldiers need them to make parachutes and strong ropes. Do you want Hitler to win this war?"

"Of course not!"

"Then stop your belly-achin'! You're not the only one who's had to sacrifice," Mildred remarked. "Even I'm starting to get tired of wearing soldier green and sailor blue. I look much prettier in purples and deep pinks."

Merle rolled her eyes. "Is that what Jake told you?"

"That's not fair, Sis! Leave my boyfriend out of it!"

"C'mon girls! Don't forget it's our patriotic duty to support our troops," reminded Ruth. "It's a privilege, and we've gotta make sure we're backin' our boys. What if Hitler came to America?"

"I'd give him a run for his money!" boasted Mildred.

"Sure you would Mid," teased Merle. "All the way home to hide in the cellar!"

The girls laughed as Mildred stuck her tongue out at her sister. Merle threw back her strawberry blonde hair and laughed along with the others. Sisters, yes, but many refused to believe the dark and light haired girls were really twins.

"Well, now that the troops have broken through at Normandy, perhaps we won't have to do without stockings and certain fashions and foods much longer," stated Merle rather wistfully.

Her sister nodded. "Wasn't that newsreel exciting? Elise, did you see anything you recognized?"

"Well, I'd like to say the beaches, but none of it looked like anything I remembered the one summer we visited the seashore. Besides, I was so young then."

Elise suddenly turned serious as a far away look came into her eyes. " Actually, I was thirteen when I came to America to escape Hitler," she said.

"Yes, I remember," replied Ruth. "We were all so excited to meet you after your aunt told us at church that you'd be coming."

"Did she ever tell you why I was suddenly sent here?"

"Other than something to do with the war, we never heard specifics."

The other girls nodded, listening and waiting for an explanation.

"Well, right before I turned thirteen, my best friend's parents were giving her a thirteenth birthday party. She was a few weeks older than me and was so excited about becoming a teenager. Of course, we all were at the time. A few months before her birthday, Hitler's forces had begun their attacks, and before we realized what was happening, the bombs started falling in our own village. We never knew when the high pitched sound of an incoming missile would send us for cover. That's why my parents made the decision to keep me home from Simone's party. Of course, I was crushed."

"Was your friend upset that you didn't come?" asked Mid.

"I'm sure she was disappointed, but I never had the opportunity to really find out. Right after my classmates had gathered in her home, a Nazi bomber flew over. As far-fetched as it sounds, it went down Simone's chimney, killing her and her mother, as well as injuring the party-goers."

The three girls gasped as they walked on in silence, each lost in her thoughts. Looking down at the sidewalk no longer sure of what to say, fashions and movies no longer seemed to fit the conversation.

Ruth slowly lifted her head just in time to see a tear slide down Elise's face. At first she thought the memory alone had been enough to sadden her friend. But then she followed the girl's gaze where it had landed on Willie, her sailor boy, who was laughing and kissing a pretty girl just outside a Chinese restaurant; they were obviously meeting for dinner.

No one said anything as they continued toward home. They didn't need to because pain had a language of its own.

Chapter 18
A Sea of Sorrow

It was rumored that the boat had been wired with explosives and would be sunk with all prisoners on board. For Aleksy, these reports brought to mind official orders concerning political prisoners: not to give them up to the allies. One way to a avoid this would be dropping them in the bottom of the sea.

The freighter navigated toward Kiel, the gateway to the Baltic. However, the Germans soon discovered the allies had arrived ahead of them and were already busy bombing the city. So, rather than docking, the SS simply piloted the ship toward Denmark .

A day or two had passed when Aleksy's Italian friend had taken to screaming day and night in pain from his unattended wounds. Infection was no doubt rampant.

"Pietro," Aleksy whispered. "You must try to calm down, or the Gestapo will kill you. You're drawing too much attention to yourself."

"I cannot help it," he whimpered. "The pain is unbearable. I'd rather be shot!"

"Pietro, you must hang on! Freedom awaits us. Don't give in! You're Italian, and you're strong."

"No, Aleksy," came the choked whisper. "I'm weak… the pain is like death itself!"

Aleksy watched the boy grab his stomach as he screamed. The area was severely swollen, even through his shirt.

Aleksy turned his head away rather than watch the boy convulse in pain. His own wound was presenting troubles enough, but he couldn't allow himself to think about it. The men around him were beginning to complain about an infestation of lice and the odor of rotting skin due to unsanitary conditions, not to mention the long hours in the direct sunlight on the upper deck.

"Oh, Aleksy, please help me! Make it stop!" Pietro's moans once again broke into Aleksy's thoughts. It was enough to send him into hysteria, but he had to keep his sanity, especially if everyone else around him was losing theirs.

"Be still, my friend! The soldiers are looking this way! Bite your lip as hard as you can whenever the pain hits!"

Pietro turned his head toward Aleksy nodding solemnly as his teeth dug into his bottom lip. Blood drizzled onto his chin, but the remedy didn't last long as he once again bellowed in pain.

Aleksy ripped fabric from the bottom of his own shirt then leaning over stuffed it into his friends bleeding mouth to serve as a gag. However, the attempt to help his friend didn't come soon enough.

Two members of the Gestapo approached the tormented prisoner. One kicked him in the side. "Shut up!" he yelled.

Pietro cringed with fear as the two men pulled up his soiled shirt and studied his wound. Looking at one another, the older one nodded. Next, they bent forward picking the Italian up by his feet and beneath his arms as if he were already a corpse. The small man could not have weighed much by the way the Nazis effortlessly carried him across the deck. "Aleksy?" he called out.

Aleksy closed his eyes, knowing what was coming. "It's ok, my friend," he called out in return. If he'd been a praying man, the heavens would have been bombarded at that moment, but poor Pietro was evidently a very unlucky soul. Aleksy put his fingers in his ears, but they couldn't block out the screams of his friend as he met his demise in the bottom of the Baltic Sea, now a sea of sorrow.

Although neither food nor water was provided on the ship for the prisoners, Aleksy, along with some of his wounded friends, proved strong enough to survive the voyage which at this point would soon end. Prior to reaching its destination, the ship's captain made a surprising visit to the men and explained, in German, that his crew had overthrown the SS Guards and had locked them up.

Several days later, the prisoners were finally given food and told they would be docking in Denmark. However, this proved to be impossible, as the Danes fired on the approaching ship clearly bearing the white flag of surrender. Evidently, they weren't taking any chances.

Aleksy couldn't help but wonder what good such a flag was if the other side didn't adhere to the rules. Even the kids he had played wargames with as a child knew that one. The captain changed course and headed toward a nearby German city which was under the command of the German Navy. He felt they would find a welcome there as well as much needed medical attention; it was the army he didn't trust.

True to his word, German Navy medics rose to the task of caring for the few prisoners who had survived not only a brutal death march but a ship transport from Hell. Placed in a hanger at the local airport which was quickly converted into a hospital, Navy nurses now battled the after effects of war as the worn and tattered of WWII clung to the leftover pieces of their lives. The once robust young Aleksy now weighed well under 100 pounds but reveled in the luxury of having beat the odds. Nevertheless, even as the realization of the little company's newfound safety began to sink in, the Nazis were not to be defeated without one last attempt.

~~~~~~~

During the night, the SS Guards arrived at the airport to carry off the prisoners they believed were rightfully theirs. Holding on to the very pride that would soon take Hitler down, their plan was to shoot and kill the survivors. However, the captain's crew was well armed and ready.

"Quick! Get me a gun," Aleksy called out to one sailor, "and I'll help rid you of the stinking Nazis once and for all!"

The sailor shook his head, "This is no longer your job; we're here to protect you now."

Aleksy harrumphed. This was a foreign idea. "I don't need your protection," he replied. "I've made it this far without your help. Now, give me a gun!"
~~~~~~~

The officer cracked the door peeping outside onto the tarmac, his gun at the ready and laughed. "You can't even get out of bed, Pole! I prefer to defend myself rather than allow an invalid to protect *me*."

"An invalid?! You call me an invalid? " Aleksy sat up in bed mustering as much strength as he could, hands tucked into fists, ready for a fight.

"You don't scare me," joked the man. "Now go to sleep while I rid the world of a few more demons." With that, he disappeared.

Aleksy crawled from his bed and painfully made his way toward the closest door of the hanger. Stepping into the cool night, he leaned his back against the metal building, then catching his breath, crept into the night using the structure as a support, his bad leg dragging behind him. Suddenly an SS soldier crept up behind him and clamped his hand over Aleksy's mouth before he could alert anyone.

"Well, look what I have here," the soldier snickered, "an injured prisoner who belongs to the Third Reich."

Aleksy twisted his body trying to get lose, pain shooting though his injured leg.

"You weren't content to die in our custody, but we will soon have you back and we guarantee death in spite of your stubbornness, Pole. Or like most Poles, are you too stubborn to die?"

Aleksy jerked his body back and forth trying to take his attacker down but to no avail. The man simply tightened his grip and laughed at the attempt.

Aleksy determinedly thrust his body into that of the SS soldier stomping hard on his foot with all the weight he could muster. Caught off guard, the German soldier yelped and let go of Aleksy who made a dash around the corner of the building wincing in pain, but suddenly came to a quick halt. A German navy officer held a gun on a small group of SS soldiers.

"These prisoners you claim as property of the Third Reich are no longer your concern," the soldier told them, "because now you're *our* prisoners. And I really don't think Hitler's going to be too happy about this."

Aleksy looked about for a gun, a stick, anything that would serve as a weapon. He spotted a shovel against the wall and grabbed it, ready to fight.

Suddenly a shot rang out, and a frenzy ensued - German sailors against German SS soldiers. Aleksy raised his shovel high in the midst of battle, flailing it in every direction like a madman. Shots sounded, echoed by the cries of men as they fell to their deaths. By the time the air cleared, the German navy had taken down a host of SS guards and sent the rest scurrying, hopefully back to their beloved regime.

Aleksy and the remaining wounded were soon removed from the airplane hanger and placed in a hospital where they continued to receive care until the arrival of the allies. It was May 1945, and they were just learning of Adolf Hitler's death. As the allies poured into the nearby cities, English and Polish as well as French and other allied officers came to visit their own. But for Aleksy, there were no visitors. He once again felt like an orphan of war.

Aleksy watched as other allied prisoners were claimed by their military officers and taken home to begin the life of a post-war veteran, whatever that might be. One by one he said good-bye to the few who could relate to the sufferings of combat and to the hardships of imprisonment - to those who's lives were forever changed. Regardless of one's cultural background, they would be forever united by the horrors of war.

The men shared their farewells and stepped across the threshold toward "normalcy," attempting to lay to rest the nightmare they had lived. It was a nightmare that many would bury in the deep dark, crypts of repressed memory. It would change how they lived and how they related to others, but most of all, it would haunt them to their dying days.

At only nineteen, Aleksy had already been through more misery than most people live through in a lifetime. Still, he was young enough to believe that his own sheer grit and will would continue to carry him through, an embedded belief he would rely upon again and again. A belief fashioned on the road to Warsaw as a fourteen-year-old. And a belief fashioned by the will to live. The SS guard would no longer be looking over his shoulder, but an unknown watcher would see his every move.

Chapter 19

Return from the Land of the Dead

The day finally came when Aleksy received a visitor from the Polish Armored Division which had landed in Normandy with the allies. His guest was a chaplain.

Aleksy recounted all that he'd been through to the astonished man of God. "You were lucky to have survived," he said in awe. Whether his awe came from the respect shown a soldier beating the odds or from the amazement bestowed upon the Originator of life and death, is uncertain.

Aleksy beamed at further confirmation of his luck. "Yes," he said, "I'm always very lucky. I was born quite smart and strong and these qualities have gotten me through the war."

"Well, now that the war has come to an end," the chaplain continued, "you need to move on, start over and most importantly forget all you've been through."

"That's my aim," replied Aleksy. "But as I have no connections here, I'd like to return to Poland and at least find my mother."

"Did you not know that Stalin has taken over there? I'm not too sure what your chances will be in locating your mother as the entire country is under his command. The allies will need your help in Germany for awhile, anyway. Actually, you'll be drafted into the military there."

Aleksy listened politely, taking the chaplain's words with a grain of salt. "Had the man not just complimented him on his luck?" he asked himself. "I'll return to Poland, Communist government or not, and find my mother," he determined.

Aleksy was finally released from the hospital and assigned to a Polish Military Occupation Unit in Germany. He and his comrades served there, along with other national forces, until receiving word that the allies had withdrawn from the war. And much to the horror of the Polish soldiers, the allies' withdrawal officially gave recognition to the Communist government over the homeland for which they had desperately fought.

Aleksy and all other Polish fighters were appalled. They felt betrayed after faithfully serving with the allies to fight for democracy. And what about those Poles who had given their lives to the cause? Suddenly they were treated as if they were nobodies and could only sit by helplessly as they watched their country handed over to Hitler's one-time friend, Joseph Stalin. This had all happened as Aleksy worked underground for the Polish Army and then served time in a multitude of POW and concentration camps for his so-called crimes against the Third Reich while struggling to make his way home. If anyone felt used, betrayed and forgotten, it was Aleksander Rostek. "How," he wondered, "could such a thing have ever happened?"

~~~~~~~

A ring of smoke ascended toward the sky as Aleksy tipped his head back and exhaled. It felt good to be an adult although he knew he had arrived there straight from childhood. He did the math: roughly seven years in Hell, but now that was all behind him. Or was it, he wondered. Seven crazy years of a story no one would believe unless they'd lived through it as well.

"Ha!" he laughed. "Seven years of good luck."

His comrade grinned at him as he puffed on his own cigarette, enjoying the breeze of an autumn day. "What are you talking about, Aleksy? This seven years of luck?"

"I managed to stay alive during my teenage years because I'm just lucky," he replied in flawless English, learned from his time of interacting with Americans and Brits. He casually blew another ring into the sky.

His comrade laughed and dropped the butt of his cigarette snuffing it out with the toe of his boot. "From what you've described, it has nothing to do with luck. It just proved that you truly are insane."
~~~~~~~

"Maybe a little, but mostly lucky. So lucky in fact that I'm going to return to Poland soon."

"There's nothing in Poland besides communists. Why bother?"

"I was taken from Poland against my will without the opportunity to kiss my own mother goodbye. The Communists at least owe me that. But what would you, an American, know of such things? Your family bid you farewell with a big feast when you left *your* homeland."

"That's not fair, Aleksy. It was the Thanksgiving holiday, almost a year into the war when my numbers were finally called. They would have eaten turkey and pumpkin pie anyway."

Aleksy tamped his cigarette. "Whatever, my Yankee friend. I just know that I must return to my motherland. But how can I expect you to comprehend this? You have no clue what it's like to be forced to spend so many years away from your own home. I'll look for my mother, perhaps she's living still."

Late that summer, it had become obvious to Aleksy's unit that the occupation of Germany would soon cease. All troops would be going home. All troops, that is, who *had* a home. For the Poles, that home no longer existed. Relocation decisions had to be made, and it wasn't easy knowing that one could not return to his former life unless he was willing to take the risks that came with it.

Aleksy's armored division would be returning to England with most soldiers settling there. Others would immigrate to the United States or Canada. However, a stronger urging continued to motivate the young nationalist to return to his homeland, regardless that it was a gamble, regardless that he and other democratic Poles were not welcome there. Other than his short visit while working with the underground, he'd not had the luxury of returning home, even for a short furlough. And now he desperately felt the need for closure. He would only believe his nation no longer existed when he saw it with his own eyes.

So, in September 1946, Aleksy, along with a small detachment of other Polish soldiers, blatantly decided to defy the odds and return to the home of their birth. While his fellow comrades may have been a little nervous over their decision,

Aleksy had no qualms. “Why should I?” he wondered. Luck was on his side and after all, this *was* the seventh year. He smiled then turned to look behind him; no one was there, so, why did it always feel as if someone was standing right behind him?

Chapter 20

A Strange New Land

Early in September, a group of young Polish men made their way by train toward Poland. They stopped in the Polish city of Szczecin where they had to first obtain new ID cards and other important information regarding their new citizenship in their own home country. To Aleksy's delight, the police sergeant who helped them through the process was a boy whom Aleksy had known before the war.

Patek reassured his former friend that he would take care of all the details for his new ID card. He then interviewed Aleksy as to where he had been while in the west and what he had been doing there. According to Patek, the correctness of the details was essential to the governing body now in place.

As the young man rattled on about the new government, Aleksy couldn't help but notice something different in his newly discovered once-upon-a-time buddy. "You sound like a communist," he exclaimed.

"I am," Patek answered. "Poland will be better and stronger under our new government. Everyone will be on the same page, and there will be no order of hierarchy among the classes. We'll all be able to maintain as middle class citizens, sharing a common lifestyle with one another. Just think, Aleksy, those uppity kids we attended school with will be no better than the rest of us."

"You truly believe this?" asked Aleksy somewhat skeptical.

Patek smiled and nodded as he stamped a document.

Aleksy's attention was distracted as he watched a Russian drive an American-made jeep past the window, reminding him of the allies' decision to give recognition to the communist government there. He gave his former friend a questioning look to which Patek didn't respond. He simply stamped another document, obviously indifferent to the whole situation.

"My plan is to return to the village and look for my mother," continued Aleksy. "From there, I'll go to the Army office and discuss the possibility of joining the Air Force. I wouldn't mind becoming a pilot as I'm willing to take risks, but I realize I'd need proper training."

"Forget it," Patek replied. "The new government is very picky as to who they will trust. And the word is that they trust no one, especially those who have been associated with the west. Sorry, Pal, you'll need to find some other adventure."

Determined to prove him wrong, the would-be pilot reported to the recruiting office anyway, where he was told the Air Force was definitely not an option.

"I don't understand," said Aleksy. " I have served my country well."

"New Poland is different from old Poland," said the officer. "You have been too long among westerners; you'll have a difficult time changing from their capitalistic views. It's not a good idea for you to be a pilot or a sailor now, for all we know you could be a spy for the west."

"Sir, I am a patriot of Poland."

"Yes, of old Poland. Until you have proven yourself in our new ways, you'll not be allowed to do certain things. However, the Army will be a good option for you, but currently, there's an over- abundance of soldiers. You'll need to wait until you're called."

"Option?" thought Aleksy. "There are no options here. These communists have simply taken control."

He bid the man good day and left the military office feeling more troubled than ever.

The young soldier was at first a bit insulted considering, his track record. But like a good soldier, he would have to wait until summoned. Meanwhile, the idea of working as a civilian for a change and simply readjusting to his new life began to hold a strong appeal. But first things first, he wanted to see his mother.

Aleksy traveled back to his home village, and this time he was pleasantly surprised to find the woman there when he knocked.

The short chunky lady opened the door and stared at her son without moving.

Aleksy smiled. "Hello Mother," he said removing his cap.

The woman stepped aside and beckoned this older version of her only child to enter. There were no tears, no hugs, no show of emotion. He stepped inside the doorway and took in the pictures on the walls and the plain furnishings within the room.

"It all looks the same," he commented.

"Yes, little has changed."

Aleksy walked across the room and picked up a blurred black and white photograph in a cardboard frame. He smiled at the boy smiling back at him. He was around twelve or thirteen when the picture had been snapped - right before Aleksy marched off for his first scouting adventure. Now, in his memories, Aleksy could hear his father instructing his son to look into the box and "give it a big smile."

"You've kept it all this time?" he asked his mother. "Even when the Germans were living here?"

"I took it with me, that one, and the one of your father." She nodded toward another black and white photograph on the small wooden table. But what do *you* know about the Germans?"

"I returned home a few years ago to find they had occupied our house. I had no idea where to locate you."

"Oh," she replied. "I was with your Aunt Doneta in the east. Her village didn't draw the Germans as ours did, possibly because they don't offer train service there."

"So, where is my father?" Aleksy asked as he returned the photograph to its original place.

"Dead, I assume. There has been no word on him, and the Red Cross has been unsuccessful in locating him."

Aleksy nodded, looking around the room once more and feeling a bit awkward in the silence that followed. "So, did he die a patriot?"

"Of course. Was there any other way?"

Aleksy smiled. "No, mother."

"The unit he fought with in '38 came looking for him, but there was no need. He'd already pulled his uniform from the wardrobe."

Aleksy was about to reply, but he was taken by surprise when his cousin Daniella, his Aunt Doneta's daughter, suddenly burst into the room laughing. She came to an immediate halt. "Aleksy?" It had been years since he had seen her.

And just as quickly a man laughing loudly stepped into the room, coming to an abrupt stop on the heels of Aleksy's cousin. His Russian uniform looked out of place in Aleksy's childhood home.

The young Pole looked to his mother for an explanation.

"Your cousin and her friend are staying here for a while until they can get settled into their own apartment."

Aleksy stared hard at Daniella. His look was one of disdain; her gray eyes welled with tears.

He turned toward the door. "Goodbye, Mother," he simply said as he walked out knowing he would never see her again, and at that moment he didn't much care.

He had reached the street when he heard his cousin calling his name. She quickly caught up with him and grabbed him by the arm, tears gushing down her face.

"Aleksy, it's not as it seems! You must believe me!"

"Oh, I believe you alright," he responded as he stopped and turned to face her. "I believe that you are no better than any traitor of Poland! I believe that it didn't matter to you that your own family members risked their lives to save *you* from Hitler and Stalin! You know you're only a plaything for him! Whatever he's promised you will be short lived!"

"Aleksy, please don't say such things because I cannot bear…"

"To hear the truth?" Aleksy continued walking while Daniella clung to him. "That you are a disgrace to your own family and especially to Poland?"

"Aleksy, it's not that way! Please hear me out!"

"Everything seemed perfectly clear by the laughter in your voice and by the way my mother allowed this in her very own home! In *my* home!"

"Please hear me out, Cousin!"

"And what a lack of respect for my father, a Russian soldier living in *my* father's house! How dare you! Your own father and brothers are patriots; you must shame them greatly!"

"Aleksy! When the Russians rolled into our village, the Germans left, and we were so relieved, but soon found out they were worse than the Germans could have ever been to us, aside from their treatment of Jewish Poles! The laughter and smiles you saw were those of survival. It's only a front to keep this Russian from killing me!"

"A true patriot would rather die!"

"I'm young, Aleksy! I want to live!"

"That's not living - the slave of a Russian!"

"Yes, and what you saw was simply 'acting' that's serving to keep me alive and possibly your mother alive as well. You must believe me, Aleksy! I tried to stay away from the Russians and not call attention to myself, but Miron took a liking to me anyway."

Aleksy stopped walking and studied his cousin. Yes, she was a striking woman and therefore, it had only been a matter of time before she was noticed by a Russian soldier. Not returning or feigning interest in him would have made it even more difficult on a beautiful Polish girl.

"Aleksy, I'm sure you've heard what they do! They often go from wife to wife, divorcing her because he takes a fancy to someone else."

"So, now you're going to tell me he divorced his wife and married you?"

"No, he's still married to his wife; I'm his Polish mistress."

Aleksy laughed bitterly. "At least you won't have to worry about divorce documents." He turned and spit on the sidewalk, "I no longer know you; you're not my cousin. You're Poland's disgrace." He started to walk away.

"Aleksy! Please!" Daniella tried to halt his steps while glancing back at her Russian soldier.

"I don't want you to risk death, my cousin, because you may not prove to be as lucky as I. Return to your Russian beau."

By now, Daniella was sobbing loudly, "Please Aleksy, please forgive me!"

Aleksy stopped once again, looking directly at his cousin. "Why did *she* allow this?" he asked, nodding toward his mother's house.

"To protect her niece. On my own, like other Polish girls, I'm prey to the entire Russian army. Your mother is a patriot, Aleksy. Don't hate her!"

With that, the girl turned and went "home" to the Russian awaiting her. Aleksy's mother was nowhere to be seen.

"A patriot?" he muttered to himself. "Nothing but a coward."

Emotions had never been a strong point among Aleksy's family, but whatever might have existed before the war had long ago been squeezed out by fear and suffering. Like the stone-faced emotions of his own mother, Aleksy had learned to bury any sign of hurt, fear or even real joy. For this reason he had felt quite uncomfortable with his cousin's tears. He preferred anger.

As Aleksy walked past the village church he had attended on occasion, he thought back to the God of the Catholics in whose faith many of the villagers had put their trust. He snickered because he could not relate, thanks to the Nazis' deadening of anything religious or Christian. Aside from any former faith, the Polish had little reason to ever believe life would once again be normal. Thus, began a hardening of hearts that reached into the very spirit of man, making numb any link to a once respected religion that had sat quietly by as its followers went to Hell and back. For the church, too, was being torn asunder.

Two months later, after returning to Szczecin, Aleksy began work as a bookkeeper at a private electric company there. The power lines had been left in a mess following the war. Everything was down and out of order due to heavy bombing by the Russians, and whatever wires had been useable, had been cut down by those same Russians and sent to their own country for use there.

Having found a way to support himself, Aleksy looked up his friend, Patek, at the local police station to let him know that he would be staying in the area after all. The young men agreed to see one another during their free time and thus, reestablished their friendship.

As the year finally drew to a close, the poverty of the area loomed large. Christmas was coming, but there was little joy to be found. With communism in place, the celebration of a religious holiday was now a thing of the past. People had been too afraid to attend church as the communists were atheists and had no place for organized religion. Besides, had they not been taught that religion was only the "opium of the people"?

There were no Christmas trees nor the excitement of children watching for the arrival of Mikolaj or St. Nicholas. While there were a few traces of secular practices, most Poles could not afford or even find the festive trimmings or toys of seasons past. The city was still in a rumble, yet the government acted as if all were well as it continued to dish out orders regulating and dictating how the country of Poland would be run.

While Aleksy's friend, Patek, resumed playing the role of what he believed to be a very important position, he was actually no more than a communist servant, a mere puppet of the state. The city now consisted mainly of people who had left eastern Poland to work in the governmental offices located there.

"So, why does the Secret Service consist of such a large office and staff?" Aleksy questioned Patek. "It seems rather unnecessary."

"Because there are very dangerous people in Poland who have migrated here. They don't understand our friendship with the Soviets, but they need to accept that this is a new Poland and simply leave us alone. It's believed that many spies are coming into our country."

Patek then narrowed his eyes and studied Aleksy a moment. "Are *you* one of them?"

"Absolutely not!" he responded.

However, little by little, Aleksy became suspicious that Patek did not trust him. And although he wasn't interested in the political deception going on, he began to have regrets about having returned to his beloved nation. Still, the reality of Russia's influence could not be ignored. Its authority seeped into every corner of Polish life whether political or commercial.

While Aleksy didn't agree with Patek's support of communism, he still liked the young man but sympathized with his acceptance of a political party that held no future for its followers. Aleksy realized that Patek's own war experiences had been derived only from the things he witnessed in his small village. Germans had taken over all the farms and shipped the farmers to labor camps in Germany. Meanwhile, Patek had remained at home as a child and worked for the German farmers. In spite of being in the daily presence of the German language, his skills were meager as he'd been instructed to learn Russian, just as Aleksy was now doing. Yet, it had proven to be even more difficult for Patek. Overall, he had been a young boy simply caught up in the demands of a world of dictating adults. He had not had to fight for survival and therefore, blindly followed their orders. For this reason, Aleksy felt a little sympathy for his sheltered friend who just didn't know any better.

Although Aleksy didn't agree with what had become of his former independent nation, he remained dedicated to his job as he awaited word of a military posting. Still, he was suspicious of the delay and believed they held something against him.

Spring finally arrived and he was starting to feel a bit ancy. There had to be more he could do for his nation than the everyday drudgery into which he had fallen. Had he not spent years facing hard challenges? And now to end up in a boring desk job like this did not seem to accomplish anything.

Things suddenly livened up one morning when the wife of Aleksy's boss stopped by the electrical office to speak with him in private. The Secret Service police had arrested her husband, and she wanted Aleksy to find out why. "Finally," he thought, "something challenging and of importance." Still, he needed to tread lightly as traps were often laid for unsuspecting citizens.

"Isn't there someone else who can go?" he asked.

"I can't find anyone willing to go for me," she replied. "No one wants to take on this task, but I just want to know why they arrested him. I'm so worried, and I have no one left to turn to. If you refuse to help me, I truly don't know what I'll do."

Aleksy remained silent as she looked earnestly at her husband's young employee. A part of him wished she had not asked; the other part caused the blood to pump a little faster in his veins. This is the kind of thing he was made for. Hadn't he already proved that in recent years?

Trying not to look too excited, the young man sighed. "Ok," he said. "I'll go to the security offices and see if I can find out what's going on." The truth is, he had a good hunch as to what it was about.

Shortly after his employment, his boss had approached Aleksy and encouraged him to join an organization whose goal was freedom from the communist party. Although Aleksy was still learning what living in a communist state meant, he knew it went against his personal beliefs of a democratic and independent society. Therefore, he didn't hesitate to join this attempt to prevent leaders of Polish villages and towns from turning away from democracy. He strongly believed it was his patriotic duty not only as a civilian but as a veteran of the Polish Armed Forces.

The next morning, Aleksy stood at the main door of the Secret Services offices. The attending guard instructed him to wait there while he looked for the personnel who could help him. Thirty minutes passed before a poorly dressed lieutenant appeared and asked why Aleksy was looking for the owner of the electrical company. The young man in civilian clothes explained that when his boss was taken into custody, the man's wife had not been notified. About that time, Patek appeared and pulled Aleksy aside.

"What are you doing?" he hissed. "Get out of here before the Communists arrest you for asking stupid questions!"

"I only wanted to help my. . ."

"Nobody asks questions of the Secret Police!" he retorted.

"That's stupid! How else can we find out about missing persons? What if you were to disappear? Wouldn't you hope someone would come looking for you?"

"Absolutely not! They would arrest the person even asking about me!"

Aleksy shook his head as he turned toward the door. "That's silly," he muttered. "How could you even support such a government?"

"Leave now, Aleksy," demanded his friend.

The seeds of foreboding were now sending chill bumps through Aleksy's body. He sought out his bosses' wife and reported that he could find out nothing about her husband's arrest as he was strongly discouraged from seeking information.

When he returned to work the following day, Aleksy was surprised to find a visitor announcing that the electrical company had been "nationalized." His former boss's private company was now taken over by the state. As far as Aleksy was concerned, the government had simply stolen it.

"That's it!" Aleksy thought to himself. "If I continue to work for such tyrants, I am no more than a traitor myself! I am better than this!"

He stormed out of his office at the end of the day and found Patek. "Just who runs Poland?" he demanded, leaning over his desk.

"Lower your voice Aleksy, before you are thrown into the local brink!" scolded the shocked Patek. "And trust me - you will *never* get out once you are!"

"I need answers, and I need them now! What has become of Poland?"

"Poland has become a new nation with new ideas and a new people! I thought you knew that! Forget the old ways, Aleksy!"

"I do not like these new ways, Patek! They rob the independence of a proud nation and beat the people down!"

Patek stood up and leaned toward his friend. "Mark my word! People are listening to you even now! Stop while you're ahead!"

"How come I haven't been called up for military assignment yet?"

"That's something only our military can answer, but if I were you, I'd leave it alone!"

"What do you know about it, Patek?"

Patek looked up as an administrative colleague stepped into the office. "Everything ok in here?" he asked, eyeing Aleksy.

"Yes, sir," responded Patek, "I think there was a misunderstanding, but it has been resolved now." He returned to his chair prompting Aleksy to have a seat as well.

The man studied them for a moment, "Ok, I'll be in my office if you need me."

"Thanks, but everything is fine," replied Patek to the retreating official.

Patek leaned across his desk and hissed at his friend, "See what you've done! No wonder they are checking into your background."

"Is that true?" Aleksy asked.

"Yes! They can't trust you for the part you played in the underground. Also, there are documentations of attempted escapes and people who may have helped you."

Aleksy sat back, blinking at his friend. His mind traveled to the kind German soldier and his Angora rabbits. He hoped he had made it home to his own family.

"At least now I know there's no need to wait on any military orders."

"I'm sorry," replied Patek. "You will no doubt be under government surveillance as long as you live in Poland."

"Then, I'll just have to leave, won't I?"

"It's not that easy, my friend. Once you're part of the eastern block, the goal is to keep you here. The Reds depend on their factory workers and farmers."

"For what reason? To feed their own dirty mouths?"

"It's a new era and a new philosophy, socialism. Everyone owns the factories and land together; this system will allow all people to share equally. Just think, Aleksy, we will no longer have the poor among us."

"They have brainwashed you, Patek! I used to think you had a brain!"

"We will end this conversation now, Aleksy. It has gone way too far!"

"I need to know what has happened to my boss. I can't just leave him in jail to rot!"

Patek's steely eyed gaze met and held Aleksy's own hardened look as he stood up and pointed toward the door, "You may leave now."

Aleksy turned on his heel and left his friend's office now well aware of just how dangerous his homeland had become. What had happened to his beloved Poland? He no longer recognized her. *This* was not Poland; it was a place of sorrow, and he could no longer bear to be a part of it. And he did not like the feeling that *someone* might be watching.

Chapter 21
A Twenty-Year-Old Spinster

Elise Cornell watched the mailbox every day. Hitler and his war machine had long been laid to rest. It had now been more than a year since the war was officially over, and America was coming back strong. The D-Day invasion had marked the beginning of the end. Although the war was over, Elise wouldn't be returning home. She'd made her new life in America. Still, day after day, she watched for letters from her parents.

She knew that her war-torn homeland offered little options for now when it came to jobs or education. Besides, she had long established herself in the land of the brave and quite frankly, was enjoying the benefits of an affluent nation. She was now a working girl, saving toward an apartment of her own, seeing there were no current prospects for a husband.

The letters received from her mother assured her that all was well. She was getting along and had even returned to church and community activities. She had high admiration for a new priest in her parish and saw this as a fresh post-war beginning. As she often stated to her daughter, "Young blood and young families keep things going."

Meanwhile, her father had returned home unscathed from his role in the French Foreign Legion; he had served his nation well and was ready to pursue civilian life once again. He, too, was involved in the parish and community affairs, reaching out to those who had lost everything in the war.

Elise dreamed of returning home and seeing her parents one day. It had been way too long since she'd felt their embrace and far too long since she'd looked into their eyes. But for now, she had to do the sensible thing - work hard and save up funds for the future. And quite frankly, she dreaded the long voyage although it had now been over seven long years since her trip to the states.

Some things you just don't forget though. One being the agonies of sea sickness.

Elise stepped off the bus outside of Crawford and Mayhew where she'd been working almost two years after graduating from high school. She was so thankful that her grades had been good enough to land her a job as she didn't have the money to attend business school, although she knew her aunt and uncle would have done what they could to help her. Still, they'd already done so much.

The doorman greeted her just as if she were of the same standing as the lawyers whose names were etched on the glass window.

"Good morning, Miss Elise. You sure are looking chipper today."

"Oh, Burt! You make me sound like a baby bird!"

"Well, baby birds are happy little things, Miss Elise."

"And noisy!"

"Well, that's one thing you aren't – noisy! Happy, yes, but noisy, no."

Elise shook her head, thanked Burt then made her way into the front office where she sat her purse on her desk before opening the blinds and starting the coffee. Once she'd settled into her chair, she looked at the list of things she'd need to do today. One thing about her job, she never had time to watch a clock.

Mr. Crawford arrived and greeted Elise. He looked a bit tired to her, but she knew his hours for the law firm could be long and stressful. And then, there was one more thing. "So, Mr. Crawford," she asked. "Any news on that new baby yet?"

Digging through the morning mail, he looked up and smiled. "Not yet, but I hope it's soon. Ann had me up all night walking the floor with her. She actually thought she was going into labor, but it was just a false alarm."

Elise smiled. "Well, at least her suitcase has been packed for the last week, so she's ready."

"Yeah," chuckled her boss, "I think if she keeps adding equal pink and blue outfits to that bag, it'll be so heavy, even the cab driver won't be able to lift it."

"She's just excited."

"For now, but when those pains start coming…"

Elise tucked her head and blushed. This was not the kind of conversation she expected from her boss. Such things weren't acceptable in mixed company. After all, a new mother usually pulled herself out of the general public when it was getting close to her time.

Suddenly realizing what he'd said, Mr. Crawford blushed as well. "I'm sorry Elise. That wasn't very appropriate."

"It's alright," the girl responded with her eyes glued to her typewriter, "The main this is that Ann is ok."

"Yes, Elise. Thank you for your concern." Not sure what else to say, to Elise's relief, he stepped inside his office and closed the door.

Elise smiled as she thought back to the time she'd first laid eyes on a woman in the family way. She must have been around four or five when her mother had taken her to the hospital to visit an ailing aunt. Of course, Elise was too young to be allowed into the room, so she'd sat with an older cousin in the waiting room. As she studied the pages in her picture book, Elise looked up to see a woman strolling into the waiting room wearing a duster and pink terry cloth bedroom slippers. The little girl's eyes bulged and her mouth fell open as she realized the woman's stomach was blown up like a huge balloon. Reaching behind her, the woman placed her hands on the small of her back and made an attempt at stretching which made the balloon of her stomach appear to push out even further. Elise stared as the woman slowly turned and meandered back down a narrow hallway. "What's wrong with her?" asked the shocked child.

Her cousin giggled. "Is she going to die?" continued the now horrified child.

"Shhh," said her cousin trying to lower her own giggling to a whisper, "she's pregnant."

"She's what?"

"Pregnant. She's going to have a baby."

"A baby?"

"Yes," responded the more knowledgeable cousin. "There's a baby in her tummy, and it's ready to come out."

No one had prepared Elise for such a secretive topic at such a tender age. She envisioned the doctor cutting into the woman's belly to remove the trapped child.

"How did it get in there?" she asked.

"God put it there," responded the older and wiser girl.

She'd looked down at her own little tummy, secretly hoping God wouldn't put one in her own belly. Why the woman could hardly move!

Now Elise shook her head and giggled as she rolled a sheet of typing paper into her typewriter cylinder. How exciting it must be to get married and start a family! Hadn't that been her dream even as a young girl? Who knows what handsome Frenchman she might be married to today had it not been for Hitler attacking her own beloved country. At twenty, she was starting to feel like an old maid. Mr. Crawford and his wife were both twenty-five and had been married six years already. It just took a long time for their baby to come. Most couples gave birth nine months to a year after marriage unless there were problems. Everyone was making up for lost time following the war years.

And then there was Mid. It was rumored that she and Jake would probably be getting married any time. More than likely, it would be an elopement although weddings were more affordable in post-war America. But the ever-practical Jake believed the money could be used for more important things like an apartment and a few pieces of furniture. At least at twenty, Mid wouldn't have to experience the possibility of being a spinster. Sighing, Elise decided she needed to focus on her work.

Happy times were here now that the war was over, and she had a lot for which to be thankful: a good home, wonderful friends, a great job… She knew God would bring that special man into her life at the appropriate time; she just wished he'd hurry up and get here - at least before she'd have to start wearing orthopedic shoes.

Chapter 22

The Great Escapist

Aleksy asked his new boss for a few days off to visit an uncle who lived further east. While there, he found out that his cousins had also served in the Polish underground fighting the Germans. However, once the Reds had entered Poland, they arrested anyone who had been associated with the underground and deposited them in German concentration camps. Aleksy's uncle had just recently found out that the oldest of his two sons had died at Camp Dachau, and he had no clue as to the where-abouts of his younger son. As for his daughter, well, Aleksy knew about her.

Aleksy's uncle shared what news he had on the world outside Poland. He had heard the Polish National Armed Forces' tactical unit was still working underground with US forces. This was enough to get the ever thinking young Aleksy's mind churning. "Well," he thought to himself, "perhaps I should try to escape and join up with the underground again. It sure beats sitting around here and being used by the communists. And besides, I'm an asset to my nation because I'm both smart *and* lucky." He smiled, ready for a new adventure, not knowing the adventure would come *only* in getting out of Poland.

~~~~~~~

Aleksy Rostek returned to his job and began to plan his escape. Based on information gleaned from the innocence of his communist friend Patek, plans began to unfold. In spite of their former disagreement, they had met for lunch.

"Are there any cases of Poles traveling to East Germany?" Aleksy asked as they walked through the streets of the city.
~~~~~~~

"Yes, there are situations in which the border is open for Polish business. Why are you interested?"

"Well, the rations and lack of certain foods made me think that perhaps we could purchase things from East Germany and then resell it in Poland. Perhaps make a small profit."

"Oh, no," replied Patek. "You are describing the black market, and the police are constantly on the lookout for that. Besides, Poland does very little business with the Germans, so it would be noticed. Then there's the foolish Poles who sell bacon for shoes. When they get caught, they are fined, but then they turn around and do the same thing later." Patek laughed. "No wonder they need a government to take care of them!"

Aleksy listened intently, nodding as his friend spoke, resenting his last statement but making no comment.

"From what I know, the biggest smuggling is between Poland and East Germany, around the city of Zgorzelec. They say it serves as a good location because the city is divided right in the middle by the River Nysa. Most smugglers find they can cross the river easily because there is so much activity that the guards don't know which way to turn."

"Well, I could use a few personal things, but it doesn't sound like it's worth the risk. All I would need is a good cured hog to make a trade. Isn't ham easily available without ration cards?"

"Good grief, Aleksy," replied Patek. "Poland has pigs dropping from the sky. It seems to be an easy thing to raise around here. But the Germans? They'd die for a taste of bacon," he chuckled. "As a matter-of-fact, some have."

Bit by bit, Aleksy laid out his plans in his mind. He would simply find someone willing to sell him a ham, and then he'd dive into the river in the middle of the city, swim across and look like any other smuggler. He just hoped he could find a small enough ham as he didn't want a dead pig to pull him to the bottom of the river. But before he could go shopping for bacon, he needed to peruse his point of departure.

The young Pole traveled to Zgorzelec by train which would give him a great vantage point to the river. And to Aleksy's delight, the city was indeed cut in half, one part in East Germany and the other in Poland. The Polish border was patrolled by two measly Polish guards and the German side, by both German and Russian military police. Oh, well, they were the least of his fears. He could speak German and talk himself out of anything.

As he studied the width of the river, the daring soon-to-be escapist believed that he would have enough time to swim under water then emerge in East Germany without being noticed by guards on either side. He chuckled, making a mental note to practice holding his breath. The longer the better as the last thing he needed to do was emerge to the river's surface just to be shot.

~~~~~~~

Finally, the plans were in order. Armed with ten pounds of Polish ham and his western soldier's book, the daring Pole made his way to a likely point from which he would enter the river and swim under water for roughly six minutes. As soon as the Polish border guards passed by, he was ready to go. Stepping to the water's edge, he knelt down to dispose of his ten pound prop when he heard the distinctive words, "Get down and place your hands above your head."

Aleksy lay down knowing to ignore the order would mean certain death. But in the process he was able to first rid himself of his soldier's handbook which would have served as proof of his earlier days in the west.

The Communist guard approached the young Pole and tapped him with the toe of his boot as if he were a dead rat.

"Are you a smuggler?" the voice asked eyeing the discarded ham.

"Not yet. This is my first attempt. I've heard the Germans will exchange shoes or clothing for a slice of bacon and I . . ."

His voice was muffled out with the sound of a Jeep arriving. "Oh great," thought Aleksy as he noted a sergeant on board. While a border guard might have granted immunity, he could do nothing now short of what his superior commanded. "Luck"
~~~~~~~

obviously was now laughing at the predicament in which a man with a hefty slab of pork found himself.

The sergeant transported his detainee to the Secret Service office where he didn't exactly receive a warm welcome. Pacing and menacingly swinging a rubber club, the officer there began to interrogate Aleksy who braced himself for what was to come.

"You are escaping from Poland?" he bellowed.

"No sir, I'm a patriot of this country."

Bam! The rubber bat descended, but Aleksy refrained from flinching.

"*Now* you will tell me! You are a spy! No?"

"No, I'm not! I'm a patriot."

Wham! Down came the club over and over until the officer grew weary, his waning strength a godsend to the boy.

"You are a German or other national enemy of the Polish People's State!"

"No, I'm a patriot who's spent years in German concentration camps."

Wham! "Stop lying to me, and admit that you are a spy!"

"No! I'm not a spy! I'm a patriot!"

"Wham!" came the club slamming and slamming until the officer once again wearied himself. Eventually he called for the sergeant and ordered him to lock up the fugitive in a single cell.

Aleksy learned from the conversation between the two officers that he would be registered for the next trip to Russia. Once there, he would be "re-educated" in the ways of patriotism, communist style. When the officer exited the room, the sergeant turned to Aleksy and clarified that he would indeed be sent to Russia in a few weeks or so - whenever the transport arrived. Suddenly, it was déjà-vu, and Aleksy felt himself being transported back to a prison cell in Germany.

No stranger to prison life, the now twenty-two-year-old Aleksy resigned himself to the conditions of his current situation, solitary confinement. For the next two days, he studied the sergeant in charge of the prisoners and decided he could easily be bought. Taking a chance, Aleksy requested that he be assigned to work duty rather than solitary confinement.

"After all, I'd be of better use to the new government," he told the sergeant, "if I'm allowed to help care for Poland. Would this not look better to your superiors?" Then proudly displaying a rather nice-looking watch he'd purchased while working at the electric company, Aleksy added, "Would this not look good on the wrist of a sergeant?"

Aleksy knew a regular prison cell would mean opportunities to get outside, thereby allowing him to return to the river and finally escape. And as his luck returned, relocation was bought with a watch that wasn't waterproof anyway, so, no real loss to Aleksy.

A few days later, he was placed into another cell with several boys and men whose job was to sweep the city streets daily as well as work in the parks along the Nysa River. Aleksy chuckled inwardly at his good fortune.

He found that all the other detainees were Poles except for one young man who was a German. A prisoner of war who had been incarcerated in another Polish camp and working during the day on a farm, he had attempted to escape to his eastern German hometown only four months earlier when he could take no more. And like Aleksy, he too was caught while trying to swim across the river. Rather than being returned to the POW camp, the decision was made to keep the German in Zgorzelec.

As no one else in the cell spoke the German language, Aleksy befriended the young prisoner, Otto, who was the same age as he. He fought in Russia and was captured by the Polish Army toward the end of the war. Meanwhile, Otto was not allowed to write home, so his family knew nothing of his whereabouts. He took solace in the rumor that he would be released by Christmas.

Once again, Aleksy's mind was in motion, plotting his next escape. He knew that when the time came, he would again venture toward the German border and any new dangers lurking there. Suddenly, it occurred to him how his new German friend unknowingly could play a part in Aleksy's survival once he re-entered Germany. Aleksy would simply learn everything he possibly could about this young German. He would memorize the soldier's ranks, name of his officers, places he fought and so on. Then while traveling among the Germans, he would have a story, an identity, something that would make sense.

However, if instead he was caught by the Russian SS, he would be able to use his newly acquired Russian language to listen to the interrogation questions twice. First in Russian, then again in German as it was translated to him. His interrogators would have no clue that he understood Russian, and this would buy him additional time to come up with the appropriate replies, something he knew he could do as he weighed out his answers from the perspective of a German soldier.

As the weeks passed, Aleksy studied all he could about his new acquaintance while waiting for word of his own transport to Russia. Finally word came that there would be no transport anytime soon as only a few prisoners were slated for the trip. This allowed more time for Aleksy to memorize the background he would have to assume in order to "borrow" facts from his German friend.

"Why do you, a Pole, ask so many questions of me?" Otto finally interrogated the inquisitive Aleksy.

"Well, what else is there to talk about? I enjoy getting to know new people and new cultures," he replied. "Besides, we don't hear any news from the outside world, and getting to know one another is a good way to build our friendship. Perhaps we will be able to keep in touch once we leave this place."

Otto nodded, "Yes, I agree, and it would be nice to maintain contact."

The following week, the inmates were told that they would be working in the park along the river. Aleksy was delighted to hear this news as it was the opportunity for which he had long been preparing. It seems that it had become necessary to cut down the neglected bushes and trees lining the river's bank. The young veteran was ecstatic with the taste of his new adventure.

As the prisoners were marched to the scene, Aleksy took in every detail. He realized that one could see the opposite river bank and the streets above it. The German portion of the city boasted a low embankment and a small sandy beach where kindergarten children, along with their teacher, played. A parallel street ran along the river. On the other side of the street a sign boasted "MUHLE" which translated into "Mill." Every so often, a man who appeared to be the miller would stand in the doorway, leisurely smoking a cigarette as he took a break from his work.

Aleksy plotted in his mind how he could get past the Russian prison guard. If he volunteered to cut the highest branches off the trees on the Polish side of the river, he could "accidentally" fall into the water, swimming beneath the surface to the sandy beach where the children played. No one would shoot at him among the children. He would then run across the beach to the mill where he'd tell the miller that he was a German soldier escaping from a Polish POW camp and was simply trying to get home. He felt sure that the German miller would be more than happy to help a fleeing German soldier.

As Aleksy studied the situation, he smiled at the coincidence of his work assignment. How perfect that luck was once again on his side. Who would have ever thought such a thing possible, such a vantage point in the midst of cleaning brush from a river bank? It was good that the intelligent Aleksander Rostek was so perceptive. However, the mysterious one who had his eye on the Polish soldier was *far more* perceptive, and was keeping one step ahead of a young man who thought *he* had things all under control.

Chapter 23
The Imposter

The next morning, Aleksy volunteered to cut the branches on the highest tree along the river. Shortly before noon when both the German and Russian guards passed by and went as usual to eat lunch, he suddenly lost his grip and fell into the fast moving current.

Aleksy swam underwater as hard as he could. As he emerged from the river on the other side, the kindergarten children erupted into screams causing the teacher to quickly gather them to her like chicks in a barnyard. Aleksy immediately reassured the startled teacher telling her that he was a German citizen who had just escaped from the Polish POW camp. Then without looking back, he ran across the street, straight for the mill where he quickly recanted the same story to the surprised miller. And just as Aleksy had guessed, the miller was more than obliged to help. He immediately stuffed the fugitive into a large half empty flour barrel and told him to stay put.

Within minutes, Aleksy could hear the sound of the German police and Russians running throughout the streets shouting orders. Suddenly, the door to the mill banged open, and Aleksy listened as the heavy footsteps of military boots stomped through the room. His every breath was mingled with the dust of freshly milled flour. It tickled his nose and attempted to tease him into sneezing, but Aleksy refused, pinching the tip end and depending on his luck to hold out.

"That way!" Aleksy heard the miller yell. "He ran up the street right past the mill! He was heading toward the middle of town; if you hurry, you might catch up with him!"

Aleksy heard the police thank the miller as they continued in hot pursuit. Still, he remained in the flour drum, not moving a muscle although conditions were less than desirable. His nose, mouth and ears were filled with the powdery substance, but at least he had breathing space even if he did suck in flour with every breath. Finally, well after midnight, when it was considered safe, the miller closed his shop and took the young man to his home, several miles away.

"The war is well over, now," he told Aleksy, "and all military personnel should be allowed to return home regardless of which side they fought for."

When they arrived at the miller's house, the man's wife washed Aleksy's flour coated clothing and put him into the attic to sleep. The next morning, the young Pole was ready to begin his tour through Germany under the guise of a German soldier.

"Stay away from the fields," instructed the miller. "German police are patrolling them on horseback in order to keep citizens from stealing the crops.

The men bade one another farewell, Aleksy realizing what a good friend the other man had proven to be in assisting with his escape. Too bad the man thought Aleksy was German. The Pole smiled at how deceptive he could be.

As he ambled along, Aleksy was determined not to look suspicious. So, he picked up a rake, carrying it as if he were headed to the fields for a day's work. Patrolling Germans passed him nodding good morning and moving on. Taking courage, Aleksy continued walking and stopped only at night to sleep in the bushes - away from the heavily watched fields. However, things didn't go as smoothly the next morning.

Trudging on with his rake over his shoulder, a policeman on foot stopped and asked for his ID.

"I don't have one," he replied.

"Why do you not have an ID? Every person is required to carry one."

Aleksy shrugged, realizing he had no choice now but to tell the policeman that he was a recent escapee.

"I have escaped from a Polish POW camp, and I'm going to visit my friend's parents in Stuttgart to put their minds at ease as he has not had any communication with them for many months now." Only Aleksy knew just how invaluable this statement would prove to be in the culmination of his charades.

"You escaped, but how did you get *here*?" the policeman questioned.

"I escaped from a Polish prisoner of war camp outside of Krakow," replied Aleksy borrowing from his German cellmate's story.

Well," said the German officer, "I'm required to report anyone without proper identification to my sergeant, so I must take you in."

Aleksy sighed but yielded and together, the two men walked four miles to the police station where Aleksy once again fabricated the full truth of how he had escaped from Krakow after swimming across the Nysa River.

The sergeant wrote everything down that Aleksy relayed to him in his impeccable German.

"You will have to stay here tonight," he said, "but in the morning, a Russian transport will come for you. The Russians now control East Germany, and I have no choice but to turn you over to them."

Aleksy mentally stored the information away as he shared it with the sergeant. Taking on the persona of a German had its challenges, but at least he would be expected to be living in that country. He would just have to deal with each situation as it presented itself.

"After dinner," continued the sergeant, "we'll put you in a cell, but we won't lock you up; as far as we're concerned, you're one of us."

Early the next morning, the two men had breakfast together as they awaited the Russians arrival.

Aleksy dreaded the encounter with these communists as he had little use for them. The Russians, in turn, bore a strong hatred toward the Polish, stemming from the early twenties. It went back to the days when high ranking Officer, Joseph Pilsudski, annihilated the red armies in the defense of Warsaw during the Polish-Soviet War.

Several hours passed before a Russian soldier finally arrived, and to Aleksy's disgust, in an American Jeep as if he were some big shot. The German police sergeant escorted Aleksy to the vehicle.

"I know you will do well, my young friend," he said. "How can you not? You are of German stock."

Aleksy smiled as he shook hands firmly with the policeman who had looked out for him over the past twenty-four hours. "Thank you for your kindness to me, sir. It won't be forgotten," he replied.

"Good luck, son. Thank you for your service in the German Army."

Aleksy saluted the man all the while thinking how humorous the whole situation was. "I wonder what he would say if he knew I was a Pole and his former enemy?" thought Aleksy. "As for luck, I'm a walking four-leaf clover, but he doesn't know that."

Aleksy climbed into the Jeep and nodded toward the Russian driver. Once Aleksy realized the man didn't speak a word of German, he vowed not to disclose that he could understand the man's native language. "Let him think I don't know a single Russian word as this will buy time during my interrogation," he said to himself.

Within the hour, the Jeep rolled into the next city where the Russian soldier took his passenger into what was left of the administration buildings that enemy bombs had missed. He then led Aleksy into the office of a young Russian lieutenant who turned to the prisoner and said in perfect German, "I hear that you have escaped from a Polish prison camp."

"Yes, sir, I did," returned Aleksy in his own flawless German dialect. "I had grown tired of waiting to be released; like every German soldier, I simply want to return home. Was that too much to ask of the Poles?"

"Not to you, but there's a timeline for everything, including wrapping up a war, especially a World War," the lieutenant responded. "However, if you'd waited a few more months, you would have been released. The Poles are planning to release all German POWs in time for Christmas."

"They are?" feigned Aleksy, pretending not to know.

"Well, that's water over the dam now that you have managed to escape. Where are you from anyway?"

"A Province of East Prussia. It was called Konigsberg, but is now called Kalimimgrad," recited Aleksy based on the information his cellmate had shared.

The lieutenant nodded. "The captain will see you later this afternoon. Meanwhile, I need to collect some information from you that he will need. So," he continued, "what is your home address in Konigsberg?"

The lieutenant drilled Aleksy with question after question as he attempted to place the "displaced" soldier. He'd make a notation and then continue with another round of questions that included the young man's place and years of service never realizing most of the information belonged to a German prisoner by the name of Otto Fischer.

Aleksy looked directly into the lieutenant's eyes as he explained in great detail how he was wounded in his left leg then taken to a field hospital somewhere in southeast Poland. "My leg was pretty bad and it took a long time to heal," he explained. "In 1943, I was sent to a military hospital and later, I returned to my unit which was retreating from battle at the time. Our regiment was taken prisoner by the Polish Army on the Czech border. We gave it all we had, but those Poles are stubborn fighters; they don't know when to quit."

The lieutenant nodded as he worked quickly to scribe the information Aleksy effortlessly rattled off to him. "Yes," he replied, " I know what you mean. I've come up against several Poles in my time, and they are definitely a determined lot."

Aleksy enjoyed hearing such a description from the mouth of an enemy. It reinforced what warriors his own people were and made Aleksy feel all the more proud.

Later in the afternoon, the captain arrived and looked over all that the lieutenant had written during the interview. The

prisoner sat still listening to their Russian conversation as the captain read over the report. Aleksy watched his face for any signs of suspicion. Not detecting any, he was a bit surprised when the higher ranking officer told the lieutenant to bring in a German woman who evidently was working there for the Russians. The middle aged woman who appeared was originally from Konigsberg and therefore, could vouch for various landmarks.

The lieutenant asked her about the places, names and addresses the "German" detainee had supplied during the questioning. Aleksy held his breath as she confirmed the information to be true.

Next, the captain asked the lieutenant to look at the man's wounded leg; Aleksy pulled down his trousers to reveal the scars. The Russian leaned over and examined the closed-up wound. This was the icing on the cake because it gave validity to a story that could have been suspect. Who would have thought two men would have a scar in the exact same location?

"So, where will you go upon your release?" the captain asked.

"Well," he replied, "I can't return to Konigsberg now that it's part of the Soviet Union, so, I'll find the parents of a very close friend from my unit. His name is Otto Fischer. We were good friends for some time before our company was captured by the Polish army. I have his home address and I'm planning to contact his family in Stuttgart. With that, the captain instructed the lieutenant to call the police station in Stuttgart and ask if a Fischer family lived there. Within ten minutes or so, the lieutenant came back and confirmed they did.

"Their son is in a Polish POW camp," he said. "However, for months now, they have had no letter from him."

Aleksy kept his expression in check. He knew that Otto was not allowed to write home from prison or to receive mail from his family.

"Alright, Lieutenant, free this soldier. Tell the German police to put two hundred marks in his wallet and issue an East German ID to him. After all, he is a returning Prisoner of War and should be treated with respect."

Aleksy wanted to cry out in victory, but refrained. He now had no doubt he could make it to the west and to freedom.

The captain turned him over to the police from whom he received his ID and the promised cash. Next, a train ticket was purchased to send him on his way to Stuttgart. Aleksy thanked the Russians profusely, marveling how easy it was, at that moment, to overlook his hatred toward them, and he then boarded the train for his all-expense-paid trip toward freedom.

When Aleksy finally reached his destination, he immediately sought out Otto's house. As he made his way to the door, he couldn't help but think how happy and surprised Otto would be to find that a friend had brought word of his whereabouts to his family. He would definitely have a good laugh once the family found out that the messenger had not been a German communist at all, but a communist hater, a stubborn Polish man who proudly stood for his own nation.

Aleksy took in the well-groomed landscape and the cottage with a gingerbread appearance. "There's probably a German witch inside waiting to throw a Polish Hansel into the oven," he mused. Immediately he reprimanded himself; now was not the time to think ridiculous thoughts, especially in light of the atrocities of the war he'd only recently come through. After all, he'd come too far to turn into a pessimist.

He raised his hand to knock on the brightly painted wooden door, yet inwardly he flinched as a certain bit of information came to his mind. Otto Fischer's old man was a die-hard communist, and Aleksy Rostek hoped he wasn't home.

Chapter 24
God's Business

Elise tipped her beret clad head toward the group of young ladies gathered around Merle as she headed toward one of the front pews. She smiled and waved her gloved hand at her beaming friend who was showing off the sparkler her boyfriend had finally given her after a two year wait. Elise wasn't trying to be rude, but Merle had stopped by her aunt and uncle's house just the night before to show off her prize. And Elise was genuinely happy that Merle would be following close behind Mid with wedding nuptials. Yes, the word was out: Mid and Jake had secretly tied the knot a good three months earlier, each returning home for lack of funds until recently. Now Mid could pool her income as a hairdresser with that of Jake's papermill pay to begin life in their own apartment.

The dark-haired Elise made her way toward the third row from the front, the same row she'd shared with her aunt and uncle since arriving in America. Sitting so close to the minister hadn't bothered her, but she still had a difficult time getting used to the informal air of worship in the church she had come to love. Strange though, how this less sacred atmosphere had actually brought her closer to God. For that matter, had brought her *to* God.

Her aunt and uncle had been elated that Sunday morning about four years ago when Elise put her faith and trust in Christ. It had happened not too long after she'd put her blue rosary beads away for the last time. Through her pastor's teaching, she had learned that she didn't need a priest aside from the priesthood of Jesus to allow her into God's presence nor did she need rosary beads to recite enchantments to Mother Mary who although special, was simply a willing servant of God. And that's exactly what Elise wanted to be, a willing servant of God.

Just as the scriptures stated, "The truth shall set you free," the truth had indeed set Elise free. There were times she still could hardly take it in. and as much as she wanted her devout Catholic parents to see and know the truth, she couldn't seem to get it across in her letters although Heaven knew she'd tried. From her mother's tone, she did pick up on a bit of disappointment in her daughter. After all, her mother's faith had been steeped in the traditions of her own family which continued to bear great influence in the European world of acceptable worship.

Elise comforted herself with the thought that it was all her mother had ever known, and Lord willing, she would see her parents again and present the soul saving gospel of Christ she had come to know as a French-American. Meanwhile, who knew what God's plans were for her? He had certainly kept her safe all these years, and she knew he had established a plan for her long ago. Wasn't being in America part of that plan?

Elise slipped into the pew next to her surrogate parents and smiled at them. Her aunt reached over and squeezed her hand before handing her a hymnbook. The service had started with a familiar hymn, and Elise rose to the occasion as she belted out the words to *Amazing Grace*. Yes, she too had been lost and now had been found. As she sang the familiar stanzas, she couldn't help but feel the presence of God looking over her shoulder, or at least that's what it felt like. She turned slightly and looked behind her only to see the smiling faces of Ruth and Mid. For some reason, an electric tingle shot through her as she smiled back at her sisters in the faith. Yes, God had a plan. She just didn't have a clue how it would all work out, but that was God's business, not hers. And suddenly, as she so often did, she felt a strong urge to pray for a man she didn't even know.

Chapter 25

Race to Freedom

The German imposter was pleasantly surprised when a smiling younger sister opened the door and greeted him. The young woman was fair like Otto and bore many of his own characteristics. Of course, she was ecstatic when informed that the stranger brought good news of her brother, but probably no less ecstatic than when Aleksy found that her communist father was not home at the present.

The young woman called for her mother who came quickly to the door, wiping her hands on her apron as she approached.

"Frau Fischer," said Aleksy, "I'm Otto's friend. Your son is alive and well, and he will be home for Christmas."

Frau Fischer stared at Aleksy while trying to comprehend the news for which she had long awaited. Suddenly, tears spilled down her face as realization took over. Otto's two sisters and a girlfriend gathered round as they pulled him into the house, giving him a seat of honor. Aleksy happily shared with them all that he knew.

"He's in good shape," said the smiling young man, "and yes, he will be home for the holidays. It seems the Poles want to play St. Nicholas."

The girls laughed with him and the questions kept coming.

"Why did he not write to us?"

"Once he escaped from the first camp, he became a political prisoner, and political prisoners aren't allowed to write home."

"How long has he been there?"

"At least three months."

"Where is this camp?"

"Just across the German/Polish border."

"Will he arrive on Christmas day or before?"

"I'm not certain; I only know that he will be released at Christmas."

"How did you become friends?"

Aleksy held up his hands to quiet the questions. Laughingly, he told them that when Otto returned home, he would tell them about everything, including their friendship. Aleksy just wanted to be on his way before Herr Fischer made an appearance. However, that was not to be.

Once the man arrived home, Aleksy found himself sitting in the Fischer's living room again sharing what he had already shared about Otto. As the excitement wound down, Herr Fischer asked Aleksy what he planned to do now that he was free from prison.

"I'll find a job as soon as I can."

"It's difficult to find jobs these days around here," replied Otto's father. "But I have a brother who lives in a neighboring town where there should be enough work for anyone who wants to work. They're rebuilding the city which was completely destroyed in the last days of the war by the allied bombers."

Otto's father stood up. "You stay here tonight, and in the meantime, I will send a telegram to my brother to come and pick you up."

As they gathered around the super table that night with their honored guest, the Fischer family looked to Aleksy as if he were some kind of hero. Not only was he a German soldier, but a prisoner of war who had beat the odds and made it to freedom. Herr Fischer raised his beer-filled German stein toward Aleksy who in turn raised his own.

"To the bravery of fine German soldiers Aleksy Rostek and Otto Fischer." The ladies raised their wine goblets in like fashion smiling and nodding at one another.

As conversation continued around the table, Aleksy confirmed Herr Fischer's communist patriotism when the man proudly stated, "The Russians were our liberators from the Nazis. You and Otto should become communists." Aleksy shuddered. He had already learned that Otto's girlfriend had a two-year-old son as the result of rape by a Russian soldier. But committed German communists had a way of overlooking the atrocities the Russians committed against innocent German women, both young and old, in the name of liberation. And he preferred to not think of his cousin Daniella to whom he had been unforgiving. Perhaps she *was* a victim as well.

"What makes you think that the Russians who have raped young German women can ever be friends with you?" he brazenly questioned the master of the house.

"In wartime these things happen," came the reply, "but one must not think terribly of the Russians because of one bad soldier."

Aleksy started to speak again, then changed his mind. It simply wasn't safe to discuss politics.

Two days later, Herr Fischer's brother arrived for a visit. Aleksy then had to return to the police station and request a pass to accompany the man back to his city. However, upon reaching the police headquarters, he requested a ticket to travel to a different location where, he told the police, he had military friends and could get a job. The sergeant readily agreed never suspecting the lie behind these plans and simply instructed Aleksy to report back each week until he'd found work. The young patriot nodded. However, he had no intention of reporting back. From this point on, his plan was to get as close as possible to the border between East and West Germany.

Without even returning to the Fischer's house, Aleksy hopped a freight train and traveled on jumping train after train, eventually reaching a farming village. Once there, he played the role of a farmhand, strolling the roadways with a stolen pitchfork on his shoulder. After two days of travel, he was finally close enough to view the coveted border opposite the city of Goettingen. Although no fences had been erected yet, there were many Russian soldiers and East German police patrolling the area, making sure their "citizens" didn't get the idea to go west and enjoy the luxury of freedom.

Taking in his surroundings, Aleksy cautiously slid down into the shadows of a ditch about 600 yards from the border. There, he waited and watched, thinking through just how he could pull it off, his great escape. It was vital that he not get caught again. This time he would either be shipped to Siberia by the Russians, or worse yet, shot as a spy.

The night was clear meaning visibility was good for both the border guards and Aleksy as well. There were lights everywhere, and the Russians had dogs. As he contemplated his predicament, Aleksy decided that if he could get close enough without being noticed, perhaps he could find an opening between the patrols, then quickly race through it to the safety of the allied side where the English would be on duty. Suddenly, he heard a noise. Someone was coming!

The young Polish man snapped his head around in time to make out four people coming toward him. He discretely reached for his only weapon, the pitchfork, and waited, his breath barely audible.

As this company of four drew near, Aleksy noticed that each carried a suitcase or two with a traveling bag of some kind. Stopping short, they too were startled as they made out the shadow of a hidden man.

"What are you doing here?" asked one in a loud and somewhat agitated whisper.

"I'm trying to cross the border," he responded.

"So are we," came the reply. "We often smuggle wares across this border. You are very lucky that we ran into you because this is a very difficult place from which to cross over."

"What do you suggest?" asked Aleksy as he loosened his grip on the pitchfork.

"If you'll help us carry one of our bags, we'll take you across the border. You'll have to leave the pitchfork though." Aleksy readily tossed it to the side of the ditch.

"We're paying off the Russians, and they'll let us through when their officers are away."

Aleksy couldn't believe what he'd just heard. Surely, if he'd never believed in angels, he certainly had to now! But smiling, he simply whispered, "What luck!"

Thrilled to make the acquaintance of the four suitcase bearing smugglers, Aleksy would have gladly carried over every piece of luggage they owned if it meant finally reaching the gateway to freedom. He took two of the full bags and began a slow crawl on his belly toward the border. The four strangers and a Polish veteran, posing as a German soldier, painstakingly inched their way toward the welcoming uniforms of the allies.

At exactly 4 a.m., the trespassers found themselves only 300 feet from the line, close enough to plainly see and hear a small group of Russian guards conversing with one another. As they paused to watch one light a cigarette, Aleksy could hear his own heart pounding loudly in his ears; his adrenalin cranking up. He watched, waiting and licking his dry lips until….

"Now!" shouted one of the German smugglers. "Run for your life!"

The fleet of men ran with all their might. The Russians were screaming! Dogs were barking, and a stream of shots could be heard blasting their deadly bullets above the noise! A huge bright light rudely beamed down on the fleeing men, and Aleksy found himself blinded by its obtrusive glare. Dropping the bags he carried, he put his hands over his eyes as if to shield them while running toward Heaven knew what! Suddenly, the light was snuffed, and in the darkness that followed, Aleksy slammed into the rock hard solid frame of a waiting soldier. His "luck" had run out.

Chapter 26

End of the Line

"Stop!" the soldier bellowed in English as he steadied Aleksy. "You've made it!"

A feeling of uncertainty came over the young Polish man who struggled with comprehending the words he'd just heard. Was he dreaming? Or worse, was he dead? His feet had quit running, but his insides were still in flight.

Aleksy's mind raced in every direction as he wildly looked around trying to focus his eyes. What had happened to the light? The dogs? The sound of guns? Aleksy looked into the face of the soldier standing before him and studied the welcoming smile then the British uniform.

The Englishman continued to hold the still visibly shaken young Pole. Aleksy blinked as reality slowly dawned. He had made it! The nightmare was over! He was finally free, and he wanted to weep. But soldiers don't cry - that's left to women and children. Polish patriots stand strong. Aleksy blinked away the stirring emotions. He was a soldier, a member of the Polish infantry.

"I am Polish," he managed to stammer, then standing taller, "and I came across with those German smugglers."

"Oh," came the surprised response. "You speak English!"

"Yes, sir. I served for a while with the Polish Army in the British and American zones after the war. That's where I picked up the English language."

The Germans passed by the British soldier, smiling and nodding a hello as they continued on their way. Aleksy gave the allied soldier a questioning look.

"We know those Germans. They pass through frequently, and we don't care. Odd thing that they passed over on such a clear night, though. They must have had something really important to deliver."

A strange sensation passed over Aleksy. "Was I the intended cargo tonight?" he wondered. He shook his head at such nonsense.

"I have to report to the Polish Military Mission," Aleksy abruptly stated in an attempt to shake the strange feeling.

"Ok. You can stay here with me until the sergeant of the guard comes. He'll take you to our border command station."

Aleksy sat down on a concrete stoop and waited patiently as his rattled nerves began to calm. Soon, the sergeant arrived in a Jeep.

"It looks like there was some excitement at the border today," he said.

"Yes sir, the usual smugglers crossed over along with this chap," replied the English soldier pointing at Aleksy who nodded at the officer. "It was quite a frenzy! It's a good thing the Russians at this border crossing are terrible shots, but perhaps the German smugglers know that." He laughed heartily.

The sergeant smiled at Aleksy. "Regardless, you were fortunate to run into these crazy Germans; the Russians are told to kill anybody who tries to escape their so-called 'Peoples' Paradise'."

"Trust me, sir. It's no paradise at all."

The sergeant chuckled then directed Aleksy to the front seat of the vehicle where he rode in quiet reflection.

A report was filed on the details of Aleksy's crossing, and then he was granted a pass into western Germany, into freedom.

"Well, Mr. Rostek, where do you go from here?" asked the British officer.

"I want to go to Munich," replied Aleksy.

"We have a bus going there daily, and you're authorized to travel there tomorrow if you'd like to leave that soon."

Aleksy quickly agreed. He had to take care of some military business.

Once in Munich, he signed on with a Polish Brigade which was soon wrapping up their service there. The French allies would now be taking the entire brigade to France as civilians. The war finally seemed to be over for Aleksy and his comrades. The realization that the Brigade, along with their allies, would not be able to free Poland had taken root, and as much as the Polish patriots wanted to deny it, their hands were tied. The Russians were in full control, and no power on earth would be able to remove them. It would take the power of God Almighty to break down the walls of communism, an act that would not occur for almost fifty years, long after people like Aleksander Rostek were stepping into the elder years. But until then, the land of their heritage would be left behind as political food for a hungry bear that could not be tamed.

Once in France, Aleksy, as well as his Polish comrades, were now confronted with the decisions establishing a new life would bring. While there were options on the table, not all would be conducive to the needs of every young soldier, specifically the need to once again feel connected and the ability to return to a life that would give a sense of normalcy in light of what some had lived through since childhood.

Immigration for the Polish had now become a given unless one would want to begin life in the new communist Poland. Aleksy knew that returning to Poland was out of the question for him - as if he would ever want to. After all, he was now a marked man and a man, whose strong desire for the rights of the people would only serve to cage him in or get him arrested or shot even if he were allowed to return. Therefore, this was not even an option for Aleksander Rostek who had just risked his life to escape what had once been his homeland.

And while the Russians had ended the war on a note of diplomacy by allying its military with other anti-Hitler countries, they were no longer viewed as friends. The west did not agree with its blended Marxist and Leninist socialistic views nor its aggressive nature in which communism was implemented and forced upon the needy population of a war-torn Europe.

As he looked at the options that lay before him, Aleksy knew that immigration to the US had become somewhat restricted because of the many Europeans who had long applied for entry there immediately following the war. And now, according to reports, chances were slim of obtaining acceptance into the "home of the free and land of the brave." Still, Aleksy was a risk taker, and considering all he had already endured, why not take one more chance? After all, luck definitely seemed to still be on his side, so he quickly dismissed his doubts.

Perhaps now was time for a young Polish man to look ahead and move on. Poland's youth had fought the good fight; they had lost their childhoods to an evil monster through no fault of their own. And Aleksy knew he could stand proud among them, a child soldier who had served the call of his nation well. But he still had one more call to fulfill, and he wasn't sure of exactly what it was. Yet with it came a strong feeling that *something* was missing.

Chapter 27

New Life in America

It was 1947, a good year for Aleksy, seeing that it ended in a lucky number. It served as a green light to Aleksy that he should pursue paperwork to travel to America for a fresh start. Being on his own meant the chances were more likely that he'd be granted immigration as compared to traveling with a wife and family.

Following, almost a year, of waiting it out, he finally received permission to immigrate. So, wrapping up loose ends, he told his closest friends farewell - one of which was a man he had greatly come to respect by the name of Cornell. A good deal older than Aleksy, the man had served with the French Foreign Legion during the war although American by birth.

"How did you ever end up here, an American?"

Edward Cornell chuckled. "Boyhood dreams, I guess you could say, or perhaps nonsense. I fell in love with the world of art, traveled to France and fell in love with a beautiful, dark eyed French girl. End of story."

"They say that love does crazy things, but I wouldn't know," commented Aleksy.

"Surely you have been in love or at least had a crush on some sweet girl."

"Perhaps, but even as a boy, my interests were in scouting and camping. Once the war laid claim to my life, my focus became only survival."

Edward stretched out his hand in a solemn handshake. "Thank you for all you did for the allies although I know you have lost so much in the process. Should you need assistance, my brother will welcome you. He lives in the city, New York. Here's his address."

The Pole took the slip of paper and carefully slid it into his wallet, thanking the man and giving him one more solid handshake.

~~~~~~~

Aleksy watched from the bow of the ship as the shoreline drew near. And just as he'd been told, he couldn't miss the proud lady raising her arm in welcome. "So, this is what she looks like," he thought as he viewed the famous Statue of Liberty. "How appropriate that she's the one to greet me although I'm not sure why. Perhaps it's a symbol of my departure from France. Perhaps it's a symbol of good luck." The young man chuckled as he tightened his collar and picked up his worn suitcase. It was November, and the late fall winds were whipping down the gangplank.

Aleksy hailed a cab which took him to the nearest hotel and then began his homework of sifting through the work certificates he'd brought from Germany and France to prove his skills. He would have liked to have had one from the electric company in Poland, but he didn't think the communists would allow his boss to give a reference from prison. This made him smile although he couldn't help but wonder if the man was ever released or for that matter, still alive. After putting things in order and into a cardboard file folder, he laid down on the bed and stared at the ceiling. Had anyone ever told him he'd end up in America, he wouldn't have believed it. But why not? He was known for his impeccable luck.

Aleksy turned on his side and drifted to sleep knowing tomorrow would be a busy day and that there was nothing to fear. After all, he had been a prisoner of war and had convinced high ranking officials to turn the tables in his favor. There was nothing he couldn't do. Hadn't his life proved it?

~~~~~~~

The next morning, Aleksy was ushered into the Personnel Office of a large textile factory and questioned by the man in charge.

"What can I do for you today, Mr. Rostek?"

"Well," he responded, "I've just come from France, and I'm looking for a job."

"What type of work did you do there?"

Aleksy showed him the paperwork supplied by his former major in regard to the tasks he had performed as well as his certificates from Germany. The personnel officer read them with interest. After a few moments, he looked up and leaned back into his chair, interlocking his fingers on the top of his desk, all the while contemplating the European sitting across from him. "So, how do you think you can fit into our factory?" he asked.

"As you can see, I'm good at following orders. I've worked in a food factory, ordering supplies for the military and then as a co-manager in an electric office. Also, my time in the military taught me much about leadership, listening and being alert in various situations."

The personnel officer nodded approvingly and seemed quite attentive to what Aleksy was saying. However, he sadly shook his head, "I wish I could give you a job, but right now we have more employees than we need. You did mention working in a food factory, so I want you to visit my friend, Burman Carter at this address." He wrote out a street name and number then handed it the young man. "Take the subway to upper Manhattan, then go five blocks east."

"Thank you, Sir," he said hurrying out the door to board the subway. As the train moved through the city, Aleksy checked the address written out for him. By the time he reached his stop, he realized it had taken about twenty minutes to get there. He emerged from the underground system blinking as the sunlight hit his eyes, and he was more than glad he'd put his scarf on with his coat as a bitter wind engulfed him. A five block walk would be nothing compared to the death marches of war, but his old leg wound still acted up in frigid temperatures. He figured he'd be in the elements roughly ten minutes, not so bad.

When he arrived at the designated address, Aleksy pushed the heavy doors open and stepped into a modernized foyer featuring a central desk. He approached the girl stationed there and showed her the note bearing the name Burman Carter.

"And what is your name sir?" she kindly asked.

"Aleksander Rostek."

"One moment while I give him a call, please."

Aleksy tried to look nonchalant while the receptionist spoke with several people before directing her attention back to him. "Mr. Carter will see you now. Take the elevator to the sixth floor then turn left and you'll see his name on the second door on the right."

"Aleksy smiled, glad he was used to carrying information around in his head. "Thank you, M'aam."

Mr. Carter's secretary greeted him when he stepped through the door marked with Carter's name. She buzzed her boss over the intercom. "Send him in," came the curt response.

Aleksy stepped into the man's office, taking in the charts that demonstrated the right cuts of meat as well as the right types of machinery to achieve those cuts.

Standing up, he reached for Aleksy's hand.

"Welcome, Mr. Rostek. Burman Carter. Have a seat."

Aleksy nodded cordially then sat down facing the man on the opposite side of a rather ornate mahogany desk.

"Cigarette?" he asked extending a gold case toward Aleksy who liked nothing more than a good smoke but was too nervous to accept. So, he shook his head "no" instead.

"I hear you're an ally from the war. France?"

"Actually, Poland. I had to make my home in France for a while after the war as Poland is now closed to us," replied Aleksy.

"Terrible thing that happened to you Poles. Well, Boy, try not to be too discouraged over the little credit you fellas have received. It's all in the politics, Son, so, I hope you won't feel too betrayed by America. Wasn't much we could do once the Reds moved into your country. Good fighters, that's what you people are. Too bad it all happened so quick."

Aleksy wasn't sure how to reply or what this had to do with a job. So, he said nothing.

"Anyway, Son, I can put you to work here; it's the least I can do considering your faithful service as a wartime ally. Can you oversee a bunch of factory workers?"

Aleksy felt a bit surprised. He would have been happy to simply *be* a factory worker but this man was offering him the position of boss. He beamed. It was beginning to look like his Polish luck had indeed followed him to America.

"I can certainly try," he said. "I do have some experience as a supervisor while serving with the allied division in France. It was something I actually enjoyed."

"Well, then, good, Son!"

He pushed a button on an intercom, "Vivian?"

"Yes, Mr. Carter."

"I need the employment forms for Mr. Rostek. Would you bring them in here, please?"

"Yes, sir."

The boss sat back and clasped his hands together. "So, Mr. Rostek, what is the most memorable thing about your time in the service?"

"Staying alive," he chuckled while wondering what kind of question that was. "Did you serve with the American military?"

"No, as you can see, I was too old when the call for duty hit the states. But rest assured, my factory did all it could to supply our troops with food and to give their wives, sisters and mothers jobs. Only thing is, I think we created a monster once these women tasted a paycheck," he laughed. "Don't know where our boys would've been without our Rosie the Riveters, though. They kept the war machine going."

"Yes, sir - so I've heard," responded Aleksy.

The secretary tapped lightly on the door then entered with the paperwork which she handed to Aleksy before turning to leave.

"Take those home tonight and fill them out for me. And since it's Friday, let's take a tour of the factory so you can see your work site. How about if you begin work on Monday?"

Aleksy grinned. "I'm more than ready, sir."

"Good," responded Carter as he stood, "let's go out to the factory then."

Aleksy placed his new paperwork into the cardboard folder he carried and stood.

As they entered the factory, the stench of raw meat and blood enveloped Aleksy. Naked pig carcasses with missing heads hung upside down from metal hooks. Aleksy's head began to spin as he looked from the pigs dripping blood to the workers cutting up the remains of their heads. Snouts and ears were being sawed into as well as what appeared to be the scooping out of brains as employees bent over their work. Cleaned and scraped hearts, along with other organs, lay along the work area. Employees' hands were covered with blood and slime as they worked.

Suddenly, Aleksy found himself in the midst of a smelly pig pen, gasping for his breath. He could smell the blood from pieces of animal organs. His memory drew up a vision of men cooking and eating the human hearts of nearby corpses. In his mind, Aleksy fought with scavenging pigs to harvest particles of food scraps thrown into the pig sty while hungry men in striped uniforms watched with an eerie longing in their eyes. The former soldier sunk to the floor unconscious.

Chapter 28
Unnerved

When Aleksy eventually awakened, he felt confused. He was lying in the folds of a crisp white hospital bed. Strange, he didn't remember his hotel room being so crisp and clean. As his eyes moved around the small room taking in each detail of the sterile setting, a nurse entered wearing a professional white uniform and creased cap. It was in sharp contrast to her olive skin and coal black hair. She smiled at Aleksy.

"Well, it's good to see you awake, Mr. Sleepy-Head," she joked.

"Where am I?" asked the puzzled young man. "Am I in a hospital?"

"Yes sir, you are, and only the best – Park Avenue Hospital."

"But why am I here? I don't remember being sick."

"You passed out in a local meat packing factory, and they brought you here by ambulance. Don't you remember anything about it?" she asked as she took his pulse.

Aleksy thought a moment. "I remember being in a pig's sty. I was hungry and looking for food, but the Germans found me there, and I remember watching men cook over an open fire. They were frying and eating the hearts of dead men. The stench, the blood…"

The nurse was turning as white as her uniform. She patted Aleksy's arm. "Just rest, Mr. Rostek. Everything will be ok. The doctor should be in to see you soon."

Aleksy nodded and closed his eyes.

An hour or so later, Mr. Carter from the meat-packing factory and another gentleman entered the room. As everything was finally beginning to come back to Aleksy, he felt embarrassed to see the man who had just employed him. "So much for that job," thought Aleksy, not that it was something he wanted to do now that he fully understood what it was. How could he have been so ridiculous? The place was a food factory – meat packing.

Mr. Carter smiled as he approached the side of the bed. "Hello, my boy. I'm so sorry about what happened back at the factory. I had no idea it would affect you in such a way. Are you going to be alright?"

"I think so," replied Aleksy, feeling somewhat sheepish. "I guess I didn't realize what a food factory does."

"Well, you're not the first. Being with a well-known food packaging business, I just assume everybody knows it's about butchering meat. After all, is there anything besides meat and potatoes?" He laughed at his own attempted humor.

Aleksy smiled then turned his eyes to the other man who had come into the room with Mr. Carter. He looked familiar.

"Oh, excuse my bad manners," Carter said. "This man was contacted when we found his name and address in your wallet; hope you don't mind that we went through it."

The other man stuck his hand out toward Aleksy. "I'm Paul Cornell. I'm not sure how you came by my address, but these folks felt they should get in touch with me."

Aleksy blinked. "Your brother, Edward, told me that if I needed anything you would help. Do you know how much you look like him?"

Paul laughed. "So, I've been told, although you can see that I'm the better looking one."

It was now Aleksy's turn to laugh along with this kind American. "Thanks for coming. After all, I'm a complete stranger to you and…"

"If you're a friend of my brother's, then you're definitely not a stranger. It's been a while since I've seen him. How does he look?"

"Not as handsome as you," Aleksy returned the joke. "But seriously, he looks well and is in good health."

The men laughed then Carter continued, "The doctor plans to keep you overnight, and then he'll release you tomorrow morning. I'll pay your hotel bill tonight and your hospital bill since it's my company's fault you ended up here."

"I don't think I can blame your company, Mr. Carter."

"And as far as the job goes, well, I'm not sure that the meat packing industry is for you – unless you're willing to work in my accounting office. Your records indicate some experience with numbers overseas."

"Yes, Sir. I actually worked in the accounts department for the military when we were helping rebuild France."

"Great! Now get some rest, and I'll still plan to see you Monday morning at nine sharp."

"Yes, Sir! I'll be there!"

"And as for me," added Mr. Cornell, handing Aleksy the paper bearing his own address, "You'll need this to get to my home for Sunday dinner. We'll see you there at one o'clock."

The two men bid the patient farewell and headed out the door.

Aleksy leaned back into the crisp linen pillow. He couldn't believe how his luck kept growing! Was this for real? A job *and* a friend already in America? Hadn't he just arrived?

As if on cue, the nurse reappeared carrying a food tray. "How about some good American cuisine, Mr. Rostek? And that's saying a lot in a hospital."

"I have a feeling, I've had much worse than hospital food where I came from. Prison guards don't offer too many choices on the menu."

The nurse set his plate on a hospital tray and positioned it over his bed. "What do you mean?" she asked somewhat curious.

"Well, as a prisoner, I was given watered down soup and a little stale bread to go with it. Sometimes, vegetables were on the menu, but they were pretty close to rotten by the time we got them."

"Oh, no! I'm so sorry," replied the nurse.

Aleksy smiled. "Don't be. It only made me stronger – perhaps not physically but emotionally, more determined to beat the enemy which is exactly what I did."

"It sounds as if you may have lived out quite a story."

"You can say that again. But now that the story has come to an end, I can look back and be proud of all I've done."

The nurse raised the upper part of his bed, cranking it from behind. "I'm not so sure this is the end of your story, Mr. Rostek. I think it could very well be the beginning."

"What do you mean?"

"Well, have you ever felt like something is *still* there? Still a part of your story, but you can't put your finger on it?"

Aleksy paused a moment as he picked up his fork. Is it possible that a hospital nurse knew more about him than he even knew? "No," he thought, "It's just coincidence."

"Have you always lived in America?" he suddenly asked.

"Oh, no. I'm actually from Austria."

"Then how ever did you end up here?"

"Three years before the war officially started, my parents had a strong feeling that they needed to leave our country and come to America. So, they began the process of scraping together enough money for passage for me and my two sisters. Then there was the immigration paperwork which required proper documentation . The plan was to send their three daughters ahead, and they would join us later. A special Jewish organization agreed to host me and my sisters so that we would have someone to take responsibility for us. I was twelve at the time and my oldest sister was eighteen."

"So, when did your parents join you?"

The nurse blinked. "Oh, they didn't. They weren't able to save up enough money for their own passage and were eventually sent to Camp Mauthausen, where they both died before the end of the war."

Aleksy grew silent. There wasn't too much he could say. The nurse documented the chart at the foot of her patient's bed then exited the room.

Suddenly Aleksy had lost his appetite. He pushed his plate away, contemplating the short exchange he'd had with the Jewish nurse. No, she hadn't faced a battlefield nor a prison camp thanks to her parents. But one wouldn't necessarily call her lucky, would they? Her parents had sacrificed their lives for her. Aleksy tried to wrap his mind around this one, even trying to picture his own parents sacrificing their lives for his, but he couldn't fathom it –

such logic just didn't make sense. Perhaps it was just unlucky to be a Jew.

The nurse's statements had been disturbing which made him feel like a weakling instead of the strong soldier he'd always been. He didn't like this feeling because it only reminded him that in spite of his good luck, there was still a missing piece. He quickly looked up from his hospital tray. Had someone besides the nurse just entered his room? Someone had to have at least stopped outside his door. How odd that no one was there, though it sure felt like it. Perhaps he was slowly losing his mind. When would this strange feeling of being watched go away? Hopefully soon – because it totally unnerved him.

Chapter 29

A Familiar Connection

Aleksy boarded the city bus with Paul Cornell's address in hand. The ride only took twenty minutes but seemed longer as he wasn't exactly sure where he was going. Still, it was good to get out of his hotel room as it made him feel closed in.

The bus pulled to a stop in a middle income neighborhood. As Aleksy emerged from the public transportation vehicle, he spotted a huge brick complex of housing apartments. "Oh, great!" he thought. "How will I ever find the right one?"

He made his way toward the front side of the building where a security guard stood checking off visitors. "Sir, where do I find C10?"

"You haven't gone far enough," he replied. "Go back outside then over two buildings. The third building over is Building C. Go inside the lobby and take the elevator to the 10th floor. You'll find Mr. Cornells' name on the door to his apartment."

Aleksy thanked him then hurried on; he didn't want to be late.

When he stepped into the lobby of Building C, he at least knew the routine. After giving his name to the security guard, Aleksy looked for the elevator and stepped inside with a bellhop. Just before the cage closed shut, he wondered about his wisdom in taking the enclosed apparatus to the 10th floor, but it was too late to do anything about it. He'd just have to suck it up and deal with it.

He focused on the closed door, and when he began to feel beads of sweat popping out on his forehead, he noticed the bellhop staring at him.

"You ok?" the man asked.

Aleksy nodded and smiled, feeling a bit embarrassed. At least another human being was with him, not like solitary confinement when he was all alone with a floor full of dirty knee-high water, an occasional rat and fat water bugs for company.

He watched the numbers change from floor to floor and counted them in his mind. "Six, seven eight…" He sighed when the metal tomb rattled to a halt and the bellhop slid the caged door open.

Aleksy nodded once again as he thanked the man then let out a sigh of relief when the door closed, and the uniformed porter disappeared. He took out a clean handkerchief and wiped his forehead. What would Mr. Cornell think of him looking like a timid mouse?

Aleksy stepped toward the apartment door and knocked using the brass fixture that hung there, a rather intimidating and ornate lion's head glaring at him. Was it an omen of bad luck to come perhaps? Aleksy smiled knowing that could never be, considering his lucky record.

He waited patiently listening to the footsteps and voices on the other side of the door. It finally popped open, and he found himself looking into the kind face of Paul Cornell.

"Hello, Aleksy! Come in! Come in! I'm so glad you could make it! Did you have any trouble getting here?"

"Not at all," said Aleksy. "Actually, it was pretty easy."

"Here, let me take your coat." Aleksy squirmed out of his heavy outerwear handing over his muffler as well.

A sweet face suddenly appeared smiling at the visitor.

"Aleksy, I want you to meet the apple of my eye, my dear wife, Emma Cornell. Emma, this is the young man Edward befriended in France."

Aleksy took her hand as she reached it toward him, and then in the French fashion, he leaned over and lightly brushed his lips over it. Emma blushed but obviously enjoyed the attention and royal treatment.

The two men stepped into the sitting room while Emma disappeared into the kitchen.

"Have a seat, Aleksy. Water or hot tea? Or how about some iced tea?"

Aleksy shook his head, wondering why Americans thought it necessary to put ice in everything. He was also surprised not to have been offered any liquor. "No thank you," he said.

"So, I guess you still have a lot of decisions to make as you get settled in the states?"

"Yes, sir," responded the now relaxed Pole. "The worst part was before I got here, pulling together my ship passage and the required paperwork to immigrate. Of course, the boat ride wasn't much fun – nine days of total boredom."

"And to think, people actually take holiday excursions on those things. Anyway, what's in your future at this point?"

"Well, as you know, I'll report to Mr. Carter's factory Monday morning and take it from there. I'm totally indebted to him for being willing to take a chance on me, especially after passing out right in the middle of his butchering room."

"He seems to be a good man and a patriotic man at that. You'll find a lot of patriots here. We all pulled together to assist in the war effort even though diabetes kept me from serving on the field."

Aleksy could hear the regret in the older man's voice. "Your heart was on the battlefield with the rest of us, Sir, and that's good enough."

Mr. Cornell beamed as he mulled over the kind comment, especially made by one who had evidently lived through some pretty extraordinary events.

Suddenly, the front door swung open, and a pretty girl with dark brown bouncing curls came tumbling in. "Sorry I'm late," she called out. Merle and Ruth had some juicy gossip right after church and I had to…" The girl stopped short, turning red when she saw a male visitor smiling at her.

Aleksy chuckled at the irony of having stayed late at church to share in a good piece of gossip. Uncle Paul came to the rescue.

"Elise, remember how I told you that we were having a guest for dinner today – a young man just here from France?"

"Why yes, Uncle." She looked at Aleksy, smiling somewhat sheepishly. "How do you do?"

Aleksy stood and slightly bowed toward her as her uncle made introductions.

"It's so nice to make your acquaintance," Elise responded. "I understand that you've been in the states only a few days."

"Yes, M'aam, and I guess I'm still feeling a little overwhelmed by it all."

"Oh, that will pass. I came here as a thirteen-year-old girl feeling pretty confused and a bit afraid."

"I can certainly relate to your feelings. I was only fourteen when I found myself caught up in an adults' world – the war, you know. Those who haven't been through such things as we have as children can't begin to understand."

Elise smiled, feeling she'd found an advocate with whom she could share her own experiences.

Aunt Emma reappeared, untying an apron that boasted bright oranges and lemons. "I thought I heard you come in Elise. I guess you've met our honored guest?"

"Yes, M'aam," blushed Elise tucking her head.

"Well how about some lunch? That roast beef is starting to make my own mouth water."

"Before we head out to the dining room, Elise, there's some news we haven't shared with you concerning our guest." Elise looked questioningly between her aunt and uncle as she waited for her uncle to continue. "Aleksy, here, worked with your father who just happened to give him my name and address."

Elise put her hand up to her mouth as her eyes began to fill. "You've seen my father?"

"Yes, daily for a length of time until I told him farewell slightly over two weeks ago."

Between laughing and crying, she was speechless for a moment before a multitude of questions began to roll off her tongue.

"How is he? How did he look? Did he speak of having a daughter in America? What about my mother – did he say how she is…?"

Aleksy smiled brightly at being the bearer of good news. The last time he'd acted as a messenger had been when he carried information to Otto Fischer's family, pretending to be Otto's German friend. Only this time, he didn't have to tell any lies or worry about escaping with his life.

Aunt Emma suggested the conversation continue at the table then led the way into the dining room. Elise noticed she'd put out the good china. This was indeed a special occasion.

"Let's bow our heads and give thanks," said Uncle Paul.

"Our gracious Father," he prayed, "thank you for all you have given us, not just at this table but in life as well. Thank you for your on-going protection. Thank you for keeping Aleksy safe throughout the war and bringing him to America. Most of all, thank you for watching over him even when he didn't know your ever-watching eyes were always on him. We give you thanks now as you direct his footsteps and especially his heart in this brand new land. In Jesus' name, we pray. Amen."

A familiar feeling passed over Aleksy as he raised his head. He turned slightly to look behind him. Had someone entered the room as they prayed? He looked across the table at the smiling French girl and felt both a mysterious and familiar connection to an unseen watcher tugging at his spirit. Aleksy smiled back. He knew it would be a while before he could make sense out of it all, yet he believed he eventually would. But for now? He was satisfied simply knowing he'd come home.

Epilogue

The old man found himself staring in amazement at the thick folder in his hands as he sat at his oak desk. Within the yellowed pages was the story of his childhood, a story that now seemed only like a bad dream or the story of someone else. Suddenly, all the horrors resurfaced.

"How did I survive those horrible months and years?" Aleksander Rostek marveled. "I was only fourteen-years-old when it all started. How did I ever have the will to live? To hide? To escape?"

Aleksander stared into space pondering the miracle of it all. "What about the German captain who befriended me? His Angora rabbits? The death marches, and the wound that should have been fatal?" he asked aloud.

His thoughts wandered to the agonizing trip on the German Navy ship where every sickly or wounded prisoner was thrown overboard. "Why did I too not become food for the sharks? "

Aleksander could feel a tingle surge through his body. The reality of his past made him want to weep as the weight of it pushed through his mind and down into his shoulders which had now become frail with age.

Aleksander's thoughts did not end there, for with the mindset of early youth, he had put himself in harm's way even after all he'd been through in Germany to return to his beloved Poland. He recalled the arrest of his former boss where he had worked in the electric company and of course, his own decision to escape his childhood home. Then there was the time he had posed as a German soldier in order to save his neck crossing Germany. And what about the miller who hid him in his flour bin? The list was endless, and so were the miracles.

Who would believe such a story when he could hardly believe it himself? Yet, in his very own hands he held the documents that proved it all. Aleksander shook his head.

His silver haired wife, Elise, entered his study. "What are you shaking your head over now, Aleksy?" she asked good naturedly.

"Just my war days, but mainly all the miracles."

Elise Rostek put her arm around his shoulders then leaned over and kissed his balding head. "That's because God was watching over you."

He looked into the light of his wife's dark eyes. "Yes, because you were praying for this old fool."

"You mean the man that was to become my future husband?"

Aleksy chuckled, "Yes, that's the one."

"God had his eye on you all those years because He needed someone brave and intelligent to use in His work."

"I used to think I was brave and intelligent, even lucky."

"Oh, yes, I well remember," Elise smiled. "But God broke you of that Reverend Rostek."

"Again, because of the prayers of a beautiful French girl."

Elise blushed. She still loved it when he flirted with her.

"It took courage to go into the Eastern Block and meet with the underground church, Aleksy. Not to mention all those Bibles you slipped past the guards."

"Yes, Dear, I *was* a little daring in my younger days, but once again, God is the One Who gets full credit."

"And don't forget, tomorrow is Maman's birthday so, we need to take flowers to her grave."

"I'm so thankful that your parents eventually joined us in America, Elise."

"And even more thankful that they both accepted Christ as their Savior before passing on."

Aleksy smiled now. "They were the family I never really had, Elise. If my own father had lived, I often wonder what he would have thought of the part I played in the war."

"He would have been proud of his patriot son."

Turning the yellowed pages over in his hands, he gazed in awe at the story they held. He still had a difficult time grasping it all.

"I long ago came to the realization that my survival had nothing to do with luck. I survived because of an Unseen Watcher that I was too blind to see." He stood up and made his way to a metal file cabinet. "Well, the grandkids will be here soon. Better get the checker board out; that's what they expect old folks to do, you know." Husband and wife chuckled.

Aleksander Rostek sauntered toward his filing cabinet to store away the very foundation of his formative years, the experiences that had molded him into the man he had long ago become. And as he did so, he was aware of the unseen loving eyes that watched him, even caressed him. The very same eyes of the One Who had kept him alive all those years and many years beyond. The One Who deserved full credit for the heroic life of a patriotic Polish boy.

Points for discussion groups

1) In what ways can wartime play a role in forming a child's personality and his or her beliefs?

2) How do you think Aleksy was able to forge ahead in the events and circumstances he encountered during wartime?

3) Which characters do you see as heroes in *The Unknown Watchman* and why?

4) Why was Elise important to the story?

5) On what characteristics did Aleksy base his survival and why?

6) How did those characteristics play into the image he had of his own father? Or did they?

7) What does *The Unknown Watchman* say about God and the details of our lives?

8) How would you have written the ending?

About the Author

Tammy C. Ferris is a former middle school history teacher and church secretary. She enjoys reading about historical events and novels based on Christian historical fiction. She also enjoys preparing lessons for and teaching her adult ladies' Sunday School class. Tammy lives in the Blue Ridge mountains with her husband who has refurbished an original log cabin at which they enjoy spending time.